**When th____
to it an____
discovered that the caller had dialed
the wrong number.**

Frustrated, Tori placed the phone in its cradle, and was about to head out to the nearby supermarket when the doorbell rang.

When she looked through the peephole, Russell stood there, a broad smile on his face.

She opened the door quickly, feeling complete when he wrapped his arms around her, his lips finding hers.

Russell kicked the door shut and showed Tori how much he missed her.

Tori totally gave herself over to the fires raging inside. She didn't want to hold anything back, so she gave herself to him freely, body and mind.

WAYNE JORDAN

As my readers already know, I live on the beautiful, tropical island of Barbados, where I'm a high-school teacher who writes romance. Since joining the ranks of those who are published, I've had people constantly ask me why I write romance. The answer is simple. Writing romance seems as natural as breathing. Not that I started out wanting to be a romance author. I had dreams of being the next great Caribbean writer, and then I discovered popular fiction and I found myself transported to strange but exciting worlds that I longed to visit. Since I was a voracious reader, I read every genre, but romance became the genre that best allowed me to escape the crazy world we live in. I write to make people laugh and cry and laugh again, and if I succeed in doing this, then I know I've done a good job.

always a
KNIGHT

KNIGHT FAMILY TRILOGY

WAYNE JORDAN

KIMANI™
ROMANCE

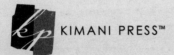 KIMANI PRESS™

ISBN-13: 978-0-373-86078-4
ISBN-10:   0-373-86078-1

ALWAYS A KNIGHT

Copyright © 2008 by Wayne Jordan

www.kimanipress.com

Printed in U.S.A.

Dear Reader,

When *Always a Knight* goes on sale, I'll be in the U.S. enjoying my summer break from teaching and hard at work on my next release, *Chasing Rainbows*—Daniel Buchanan's story.

Always a Knight ends THE KNIGHT FAMILY TRILOGY, and I've enjoyed writing each of these stories. Of course, this is not the end of the Knight family. As I've promised, I plan to write stories about Troy, George and Jared. I'm now intrigued by Dr. Jake Matthews, Tori's brother, so maybe he'll also get his own story. Expect to see cameos from all your favorite characters in my upcoming books.

I hope you enjoy *Always a Knight*. I always thought that the writing process gets easier, but *Always a Knight* was a difficult story to write. But I've forgiven the characters who kept me on my toes and took me to places I hadn't planned on going.

As always, I thank you, my readers, for your wonderful support, and hope that you continue to enjoy the stories I write. Write me at author@waynejordan.com or visit my Web site at www.waynejordan.com.

Blessings,

Wayne J

I'd like to dedicate this book to my darling cousin,
Lynn-Marie Erica.
You are a young woman of immense strength
and courage.

To my aunt, Betty. I definitely didn't forget you!
Thanks for your encouragement and unwavering support.

To my colleagues and friends, Renee,
Caroline, Gloria and Shelly.
Thanks for your help in a time of need.

Finally, to my many fans in Barbados.
You're all very special.

God Bless You All.

Chapter 1

The first time Victoria Matthews met Russell Knight, she fell hopelessly and completely in...lust.

Maybe it was the neat dreadlocks that flowed down his back, or the firm muscular body hugged by the close-fitting shirt he wore.

Or maybe it was his eyes. Two startling dark pools that held secrets but flamed with the mutual desire reflected in hers.

What she did know was that she wanted him.

When she saw the responding heat in his eyes, she knew that something unexpected had taken place in the moment when their eyes had met, caressed and lingered.

She stood erect as her mother had taught her, but

she felt the sudden urge to discard that image and do what was necessary to get what she wanted… and what she wanted was the sexy man who'd just walked into the club where she performed each night.

When she climbed the steps to the stage for her final set that night, she knew that she would be singing to him.

She'd chosen her songs carefully for the crowd that filled the club on Friday nights. But they were perfect for what she had planned. She'd always been cautious about the men who frequented the bar. However, when she'd seen *him* chatting with her boss, Rachel, during her first break, she'd been intrigued enough to ask about him when Rachel came to tell her it was time for her next set…something she didn't usually do.

Russell Knight. The name Rachel had given her. Twenty-seven, a reporter at the *New York Times*… and single. She would discover everything else she needed before the night was over. Until then she had to earn a living.

Taking the cordless microphone from the stand, she raised it to her mouth and closed her eyes, trying to calm the familiar butterflies in her stomach.

But as happened each night, when she sang the first note, the apprehension was quickly gone and she soon felt the rhythm of the music as it flowed within her.

Her first selection was a haunting melody she'd

written long ago, when a man had played with her heart and left her in pain.

She loved the song, and so did the audiences. Not because it was technically one of her best compositions, but because it reminded her of her need to remain in control of her life.

For a while, the man in the audience was forgotten and Tori immersed herself in her performance.

Russell loved music. He couldn't remember a time when music didn't play an important part in his life, so when his friend Rachel Allen had invited him to her club to hear the new band and the lead singer that she raved about, he couldn't pass up the opportunity.

He remembered clearly the mornings at home in Barbados when he'd wake up and the only thing he could think of was the feel of the steel pan beneath his hands.

But he never knew that music could be such an erotic experience until the singer lifted the microphone to her mouth and started to sing.

Her voice reminded him of the satin warmth of his island home.

The song she sang was a haunting melody of lost love. For some reason, he wondered if she'd loved and lost. He'd not had much experience with love.

Yeah, he loved sex and loved women, but that was it.

He smiled, remembering his twin sister's words

the last time they'd spoken. "You laugh all you want. Your turn is coming next."

He continued to laugh, knowing that what she said was far from reality. He had no intention of getting married. He was happy for his sister, Tamara. She'd been married for almost three years now to Kyle Austin, former West Indies cricketer.

Shayne, his older brother, had also found his true love and was happily married. Several of his sister-in-law's paintings hung in his apartment building.

In moments of weakness, he wondered if he would ever find a love like theirs, but because marriage was not in his immediate plans, he doubted it. He did know that his next lover was standing right before him.

She'd changed to a sexy number, taking the white shawl from around her shoulders to reveal smooth arms and a dress cut just above the slight swell of her breasts.

This time she moved among the audience, enchanting everyone with her passion, making each of them think she was singing directly to them.

When she stood before him, he felt himself tremble as he inhaled the faintest hint of flowers. She didn't seem like the flowery type. She should be wearing something bolder, fiery.

He didn't expect this powerful a reaction to a woman he didn't know.

And then he noticed it. The slight trembling of

her hand on the microphone, and the look of wonder in her eyes.

She'd not expected it, either.

For a moment she stumbled on her words, but she quickly regained her composure, returning to the professional songstress that swayed the crowd.

But he'd confirmed all that he wanted to know.

She wanted him. He could feel it in every note she sang, and as inevitable as the sun's rising in the morning, he knew he would have her.

By the end of the forty-five-minute set she'd totally mesmerized him. Not only with her singing, but also with the way she interacted with the audience.

Depending on the song, she was funny at times, keeping the audience in stitches, and other times she was teasing and flirtatious. But whatever the mood, the audience enjoyed her.

When the final note of her last number for the night faded, she bowed. The audience stood to applaud her.

The scent of the fragrance lingered and he inhaled deeply. Below his belt his arousal remained hard and powerful. He didn't like the discomfort but he had no control over what he was feeling.

Breathing deeply he willed his thoughts back to the stage, feeling a tightness in his chest when she bowed again to the audience and thanked everyone for coming. She blew a kiss and then disappeared.

He quickly took one of his business cards from his pocket, scribbled on it and beckoned a waitress.

Good, he wanted to see how Tori would respond to his invitation.

What he'd done was not in keeping with the kind of person he was, but he didn't want to miss the opportunity to meet her. Of course, he could easily ask Rachel to introduce the two of them, but since Rachel continued to indicate her interest in him, he didn't want to cause any conflict there.

So he'd just sit here for the next few minutes to see how she'd respond.

When Tori entered the dressing room, she headed straight for the single couch and immediately lowered herself into its comfort.

The memory of the way Russell Knight had looked at her made every nerve in her body tingle.

She wondered if he had already left. She would have loved to meet him, but some things were not meant to be.

A knock at the door forced her from her musings and she pulled herself together. She stood, headed to the door and opened it.

Disappointment washed over her.

It was Tricia, one of the waitresses, bringing her the usual after-performance coffee.

When Tricia placed the tray on the table, she smiled and indicated something on it.

A stark white business card beckoned Tori.

Her heart stopped.

She turned to Tricia and smiled. "Thanks, Tricia. You have a great night. I'll see you on Tuesday night."

"You enjoy your nights off and make sure you get some rest."

"I will," Tori replied.

When Tricia left the room, Tori reached for the card. The message on the back of the card was simple: *I'll wait for you in the lounge. R.K.*

She smiled. The nerve of the man. Did he actually think she'd respond to such an invitation?

But he knew beyond a shadow of doubt that she'd go with him.

Tori slipped her dress off and placed it on a hanger before hanging it next to several of her gowns that needed to be laundered. One of Rachel's staff members would take care of that.

In the mirror she caught a glimpse of herself. She knew she was attractive. Some would even call her beautiful. She didn't think she was, but she knew she was more than passable.

Sitting, she wiped the makeup from her face, preferring to allow her skin to breathe. She wore makeup only onstage.

Tori took a quick shower, all the while wishing that she'd brought something more attractive than a T-shirt and a faded pair of jeans.

Well, the outfit would have to do. Maybe seeing

her like this instead of the illusion of the beautiful singer would bring him to reality, but somehow she doubted that he would react other than with the promise she'd seen in his heated gaze.

It seemed there would be no way out of what she was about to do. Maybe she was being crazy. Maybe she should tell him she'd join him for a drink, but that was it.

But she wanted to experience that tingling of awareness and the sweep of fire that had raced its way through her body as he'd devoured every inch of her while she sang.

Minutes later when she exited the room, her heart beating fast, she walked toward her destiny.

Outside, the cold fall air forced Russell deeper into the coat he wore. He would never grow accustomed to the coldness of fall and oncoming winter. At times like these he longed for the warmth of his island paradise. But there was no returning to Barbados anytime soon.

The situation with his brother Shayne was far from being resolved. Quickly, he pushed those thoughts to the back of his mind. At the moment the beautiful woman he planned to make love to tonight had tantalized him with her song and earthy scent.

Russell saw her as soon as she walked out of the building. Though she was wearing black jeans and a pale blue T-shirt, she was as beautiful as if she were wearing that same stunning gown she'd worn. In fact, she was even more beautiful. He felt his heart quicken. Liquid heat raced through his body.

"Thanks for coming. I didn't think you would."

"And miss a date with the most handsome man I've seen in years?"

He tried not to blush but he liked her honesty.

"You're ready to go?" he asked.

"Whenever you are. So, where are you taking me?"

"I'll let it be a surprise," he replied, taking her arm and heading to a red Corvette parked on the side of the street.

When they reached the car, he opened the passenger side and made sure she was comfortable before he circled the car and took his own seat.

As the car pulled away from the curb, he asked, "Music?"

"Yeah, but something soft and soothing. I'm beat."

The soothing voice of India.Arie was a good choice. She said, "That's perfect. You have good taste in music."

"I'm glad you're pleased." For a moment he could feel her eyes on him. Assessing, analyzing.

"So, *you* are Russell Knight," she said. *She knew his name.*

"Yeah, I'm Russell."

"I like your work. Deep and probing." *And his work, too. Interesting.*

"I saw Rachel talking to you when you arrived. I asked who you were. Hope you don't mind?"

"No, no problem. I met her a few months ago when I was doing the piece on restaurants in New York. She was a source of help."

"She's interested. She may not like the fact that we're going out. I don't want to step on anyone's toes."

"I've made it quite clear to Rachel that we can only be friends. I haven't given her any encouragement. I'm not about relationships."

When she sighed, he realized what he'd said.

"I didn't mean it that way," he said.

"I know, but my sentiments exactly. Let's not worry about complications and just enjoy each other. I feel like a large burger with bacon and cheese, lots of onions and pickles."

"Now, that's my kind of woman. All women seem to want to eat these days is salads."

"I like the occasional salad, but I keep trim by working out three or four times in the gym each week. Not that I eat badly but I enjoy good food."

"There's a great restaurant a few blocks away that does the greatest burgers. I go there often."

"If it's Gwen's you're talking about, then I'm completely in your hands."

"Good, Gwen's it is."

For a while they rode in silence, until Russell said, "You have a lovely voice."

"I'm glad you enjoyed the show."

"But you're better than that. You're better than just singing in a club," he added.

"So I've been told. I do have a demo in the hands of a major studio. One of the studio's scouts came to the club a few months ago. I hope something good comes of it."

"So you want the big break."

"Who doesn't? I love singing at the club, but I've wanted more for a long time. Not for the money, but I want to share my music with the whole world."

"I can promise you that you will."

"I wish I were as confident as you are. It's been almost four weeks and I haven't heard anything yet."

Russell turned into the restaurant's parking lot and came to a stop. "We can continue this conversation inside. Your story is intriguing."

"As long as I don't become the subject of one of your articles, I'll be fine."

"I promise you it won't happen. Just dinner talk…to get to know you."

"Good. As long as we have an understanding. If I do get a deal I'll give you an exclusive."

"Perfect. But let's not spend the rest of the night sitting here. I'm hungry."

He escorted her from the car and together they walked to the brightly lit building that housed the restaurant.

When they entered, the hostess at the door immediately greeted Victoria with a generous hug.

"Victoria, you haven't visited us for a while.

And with a handsome young man, at that." She turned to Russell. "Welcome to my humble establishment. It is good you bring Tori back to us. She gets caught up in her music and has no time to come eat with her friends."

"I've been here before, but I haven't been in a while," he replied.

"Then I must say welcome back to you. But duty calls. I'll get one of the hostesses to seat you. I hope you enjoy your meal."

"I'm sure we will," he said.

"Good, I'm sure Tori will take care of you, so you're in capable hands," she said, with a twinkle in her eyes.

"Then, I'll have to put myself wholly and solely in her hands."

"Good, your hostess is here. Enjoy your meal," she said as they walked away, the knowing smile still on her face.

That night lying in bed, Russell could still taste the honey of Tori's lips. He knew sleep would not come easy. His desire for her went deeper than he had expected.

Of course, he desired her, but there were things he already liked about her.

The way she seemed to enjoy life and the laughter that came with it; laughter that started inside and animated her face while her whole body expressed her delight.

He also enjoyed talking to her. She was witty, articulate and had a wonderful sense of humor.

She possessed an intelligence that manifested itself in an ability to converse about anything from the arts and sports, to politics and even classical literature.

It didn't surprise him when Tori told him she had an undergraduate degree in music with a minor in linguistics, and that she was currently taking graduate studies in music.

Even now, he could hear her passion for her music when she talked about singing and composing.

She had not failed to enchant him during dinner. And she had worked her final magic on him when he'd taken her to the door of her apartment and kissed her good-night.

His reaction to the kiss had startled him. Oh, she knew that he desired her, but the intensity of his response to her almost knocked him off his feet.

It had been one of those tentative, getting-to-know-you kisses—a cautious meeting of lips that had somehow transformed into a tangle of tongues and groans of desire.

He still didn't know how and why he'd brought it to an abrupt end. He'd pulled away from her and said a hasty good-night before getting into his car and driving away as fast as he could.

He didn't like what had happened.

The kiss had been more than a kiss and he was scared.

Tori Matthews had him thinking about things he didn't want to think about. She exuded a powerful magic.

His troubled thoughts confused him and he felt the need to talk to his sister, Tamara, but now that she was married he was reluctant to call so late.

Without warning the phone rang, drawing him out of his musings.

Tamara.

He had no doubt it was his sister.

He picked the phone up. "Yes, Tamara, what do you want?"

"Is that the way to greet your favorite sister?" she scolded.

"You're my only sister."

"Yeah, but that doesn't mean anything. I'm still your favorite," she said.

"Okay, let's not argue semantics. That's not why you called. So, how's everyone in Barbados?" he asked. He missed his family.

"Oh, things are great. We just missed being hit by a hurricane. The second for the season."

"I didn't realize. I should have called."

"You always promise to call. I'm beginning to think I've done you something wrong. We used to be able to talk about anything, but now…I don't know."

He could hear her sadness. A wave of guilt washed over him. "I'm sorry."

"Is it Shayne?"

It didn't make any sense lying. His sister would know.

"That's part of it," he eventually said. "Things didn't go too well the last time I visited. He wants me back home, but only so he can control my life."

"Shayne loves you, Russell. You owe him that much."

"To control my life?" He tried to suppress the anger shimmering beneath the surface.

"Of course not. I mean you owe him your love. He's always been there for us."

"I know, Tamara, but I can't let him dictate who I am or what I do. Ever since I got my locks, his attitude toward me has changed. He didn't want me to come to the U.S. to study. He didn't want me to do journalism."

"But he let you go. He has always supported you."

"True, but only because he feels it's his duty. I know exactly how he feels about all I've done. I came home almost three years ago for your wedding and all I got was his questioning everything I've done." Russell sighed. "But let's change the subject. I just don't want to talk about Shayne right now."

When there was no response, he asked, "How's that famous husband of yours? When is his next book out? You must tell him how much I enjoyed his last one."

"It's out in a year. Kyle just submitted the final manuscript."

"And how's the baby doing?" he asked. He wasn't sure, but he felt the new life.

"How did you know?" Tamara asked, and then paused. "I should know better than to ask a question like that. I'm three months pregnant."

He could hear the attempt to control her excitement.

Russell was happy for Tamara. The maturity in her voice never ceased to amaze him. Married and soon to be a mother.

"You mean I'm an uncle again. I'm definitely going to have to come home when the baby's born." He paused.

"I was hoping you'd say that. But I have more news for you."

"What's that?"

She paused again. "Not baby. Babies—twins."

"Tamara, trust you to do things in a big way."

"So, what about you? Any special woman?"

He hesitated, not sure what to say. An image of a beautiful torch singer flashed in his mind.

No sense lying to his sister.

"Sort of," he replied.

"Sort of?"

"Yeah, I met someone. Only met her tonight. She's a singer."

"Sounds like you think she's more than nice. You're almost choked up," she said.

"Tamara, this is the craziest thing. I met this singer, and can she sing! But I've never reacted to a woman like this before. I'll have to deal with these feelings as each day comes, but I know I'm not ready for commitment."

"Russell, I know one thing. We Knights have a strong capacity for love. I'm still amazed at how much I love Kyle and I see the same intensity of feeling whenever Shayne looks at Carla. My advice, take things easy."

"What you say makes sense. I'll take things easy, one day at a time, and see where it goes from there."

"Russell, things will be fine. If it's meant to be, it'll work itself out."

"I hope it does. I'm not sure I like feeling like this."

There was silence and then Russell asked, "But you're really fine with the pregnancy?"

"Yes, I just need to be careful. When I miscarried, I was devastated, but it was no fault of mine. Just nature taking charge. The doctor says that everything looks fine."

After that he steered the conversation away from Tori Matthews.

Later, however, when he switched the television off after watching one of his favorite sci-fi movies, the image of Tori Matthews had fixed itself in his mind's eye and he wondered what he was going to do if he didn't make love to her soon.

On the other side of the city, Tori, too, lay in bed. She had enjoyed the night. Russell Knight was an extraordinary man. A man with passion and fire.

He scared her. Scared her because he threatened to shatter her comfortable, well-structured existence.

And she didn't like it one bit.

But Tori knew that their coming together was inevitable. She wanted to be sure that she wasn't making a mistake. She wasn't ready for commitment or marriage, but Russell made her think of forever, and maybe for this reason alone she ought to run in the other direction.

She had so many plans for herself. Her music was the most important thing in her life, so she had no intention of letting anything or anyone distract her. She'd come too close to her goal of signing with one of the leading labels in New York. Her agent had contacted her to let her know that the president of RIC Records had called and was definitely interested, and they were in the process of working on the details of the offer.

Tori reached for the book she was reading and flipped to the page she'd gotten to. Two minutes later, she closed the book, unable to focus on the story unfolding.

She'd made up her mind. She would go out with him when he called. Where was this leading? She wasn't sure and maybe for once in her life she could do something daring and exciting.

Yes, they would make love in time. Maybe they'd become lovers. The possibility was there, but most important was that she didn't allow herself to fall in love. She didn't have the time for love.

A fast, curl-your-toes lover would be fine. And Russell Knight seemed the perfect candidate.

What people said about men from the Caribbean was one thing, but she wanted to discover the truth for herself.

Slowly she drifted to sleep, and this time the man in her dreams was no faceless hero, but a man with dark deep eyes and hair that swirled and flowed around him.

Chapter 2

Two days later, Tori finally received a call from Russell. During that time, she'd often found herself staring at the telephone, hoping he would call. She wondered if she'd scared him off.

On Sunday, a day she rarely did anything but relax with a good novel, the strident jarring of the phone broke the tranquillity of the lazy morning.

Laying the book down, she reached over to cautiously pick up the handset. Her mother's weekly call. She sighed, knowing that she faced at least an hour of meaningless chitchat.

"Hi, Mom," she said.

"I've been called many things, but never 'Mom.'" Russell's husky voice came across the line.

Tori almost fainted in embarrassment.

"I'm sorry, Russell. My mom usually calls at this time on Sundays."

"No need to apologize," he said. "I hope I didn't wake you."

"You didn't. I've been up for a while."

"I just wanted to call to apologize for not calling before. I was in the office all day yesterday working on a story. Didn't want you to think I forgot you. Can you forgive me?"

When she didn't answer, he said, "So you're not going to make this easy for me, are you?"

"I shouldn't make it easy," she said, "but I do forgive you."

"Good, because I called to invite you out to dinner. However, I'll be doing the cooking, so I'll understand if you decline," he said.

"Now, how can I refuse your invitation? And you're cooking? I'm intrigued. Don't know many men who cook."

"Well, I promise you, you're in for a treat. I learned from the best, so I can't let her down. Get a bit of paper and I'll give you directions to my home."

"Okay, go ahead."

She wrote the information he gave her and said, "Thanks for the invitation. I'm looking forward to the evening."

"And thanks for accepting the invitation," he responded. "I have to go into work for a few hours this morning. I should be finished making dinner by seven o'clock, so you can come anytime after. I'll see you then."

Tori heard the click of the phone. She remained motionless for the next few minutes before she picked the novel up and started to read again.

An hour later, when she placed the book on the dresser, the smile on her face had broadened. Maybe she could try some of the stuff she'd been reading about.

Dinner? Definitely, but she could not help but wonder what he had planned for dessert.

At seven o'clock on the dot, the chime of the doorbell announced Tori's arrival. Good, she was on time. He loved a woman who knew the value of timeliness. One of the things his brother had instilled in him was that being late showed a lack of respect for the other person's time. Tonight, he planned on using the time wisely.

Russell untied the apron he wore and wiped his hands on the towel on the counter.

He was all done and looking forward to a quiet night with the beautiful Tori Matthews.

Russell walked to the front door and opened it. He hoped his broad smile hid the tension and anticipation he was feeling.

She stood there and it took all his willpower not to tear off her coat and take her right there on the floor. She was so damn beautiful.

For a moment he lowered his eyes and wondered if he revealed too much about the desire he felt.

When he looked up, she smiled; one of those knowing smiles that irritated him.

"I never saw you as one to be shy," she said. Her eye held a twinkle.

"Me? Shy?" He stepped back, allowing her to enter the house. "I don't have a shy bone in my body. Cautious? Yes. But shy? Definitely not." He helped her out of her coat, trying not to breathe too deeply when he saw the red dress she wore. Red was now his favorite color.

"I don't want it to seem as if I'm taking things too fast," he said.

"Too fast?"

"Yes, too fast. This thing that's happening between us… that's making me act so out of character. I'm sure you feel it, too," he said.

"Well, no point denying the inevitable."

"No point."

"So, what's on the menu for tonight?" she asked.

"Oh, I don't want to spoil the surprise. Can I offer you a glass of wine? Red or white?" he asked.

"Thank you," she replied. "White would be fine."

"Make yourself comfortable. I'll be back in a flash."

He welcomed the brief distance from Tori; it gave him a reprieve to calm his racing pulse.

He took his time pouring the two glasses of

wine, hoping that the erection that pressed against his jeans didn't cause him any embarrassment.

When he returned to the sitting room, she stood on the balcony that overlooked the city.

He loved New York, and whenever he looked out on the city, he knew what appealed to him. The bright lights that flickered all night long like fireflies and the hustle and bustle that never seemed to cease.

When he entered the room, Tori turned to him, took the glass that he offered and immediately raised it to her lips.

Lips that held a promise.

He reached for the glass, taking it from her, and turned to rest it on a nearby table.

Russell stepped toward her and captured her lips in a kiss that caused him to moan out loud with his need for her.

Tori pressed against him, demanding a willing partner, and whatever reservations he had about this tasty appetizer dissipated. He wanted more than just a mere kiss, a mere meeting of lips and a rush of passion. He wanted to feel her completely.

In his mind's eye he saw them tangled in bed, and he knew that before the night was over, he would be deep inside her.

Russell pulled away from Tori reluctantly, knowing that if he didn't he would take her now and to hell with dinner.

"I always thought dessert came afterward," she commented, laughter in her voice.

"I promise you there'll be more dessert. For now, it's time to eat. I haven't eaten much for the day and didn't want to eat just before I started cooking, so I'm ravenous."

"So am I," Tori responded, the double entendre evidence of her own need. "So am I," she repeated.

Seated at the dining table, Tori couldn't help but show her contentment. Dinner had been excellent, heavenly. Where had Russell learned to cook so well?

"Our housekeeper Gladys taught me," he responded. Tori didn't realize she had asked the question out loud.

"I must say that I'm totally impressed. You cook better than any of my girlfriends. Better than I do," she said.

"I appreciate the compliment. I always aim to please. Do you think that you can eat dessert right now?"

"I can't eat another bite. Let's leave the dessert for later. I would like another glass of wine."

"That's my plan. We can go out on the patio and chat for a while, listen to music."

"That'll be fine," she replied.

"Anyone in particular you like?" he asked.

"I'm in the mood for some Anita Baker, but I'm not sure you'll have her music."

"Not have Anita? That would be sacrilege."

"Now, I can see you're going to be the kind of man I like."

"Girl, I love me some music, so I'm sure you'll find everything in my collection."

Tori followed him. He led her into a room just off the dining room. She looked around in amazement. A typical man's hideaway. In one corner were an entertainment center and a stand with miles and miles of CDs. In another corner were a computer and all the latest technological gadgets, and on one side of the room a bookshelf overflowed with books. The only other thing was the most comfortable-looking sofa Tori had ever seen.

"Have a seat, I'll get Anita crooning," he told her and she immediately headed for the sofa.

Heavenly.

She could easily fall asleep here.

The strong sultry vocals of Anita's "You Bring Me Joy" soon floated from the speakers, which were placed strategically around the room.

"I'll be back in a minute. I'll bring dessert. You like cheesecake?"

"Love it," she replied.

When he left the room she continued her visual tour and tried to reconcile the room with the man she'd met.

This was another level of who he was she found interesting and intriguing.

Russell was very much a man, but there was

something boyish and roguishly endearing about this room.

Yes, she could tell he loved music, but the game console and the copies of some of the more popular video games hinted at the boy inside of him.

Ironically, she was as much a video-game fanatic as he was. A girl couldn't grow up with a brother and not master the skills and dexterity of the video-game fantasy worlds.

When Russell returned a few minutes later, he was surprised to see her browsing through his collection of video games.

When he handed her the cheesecake, she turned to him, a smile on her face. "You have all my favorites here."

He was surprised. She played video games?

"I do?" He didn't know how to respond.

"Yes, I just completed *Prince of Persia: The Warrior Within*. What level have you reached?" she asked.

He didn't think that talking to a woman about video games could be sexy, but at the moment, he could only think of doing something really wicked to her. And the way she was eating the cheesecake did little to keep things under control.

At this precise moment, he wanted to kiss her, to touch her.

Russell realized that she had stopped talking.

When he looked at her, she was staring at him, her desire evident.

He moved toward her, already tasting the honey of her lips.

When his lips touched hers, a coiled spring released itself.

Her body moved toward his until her breasts rested against his chest. His hands itched to touch her.

"I want to make love to you," he whispered in her ear.

"So what are you waiting for?"

Russell heard the laughter in her voice. He admired her boldness.

"So you're laughing at me?" he asked against her lips. He didn't want to talk. He just wanted to love her.

"No, I'm definitely not laughing at you," she replied.

"Come, let's go somewhere where it's a lot more comfortable."

Tori immediately thought of the couch, but that would have to be another time.

He didn't wait for her response, just bent and lifted. She wrapped her arms around him, resting her head on his shoulder.

"Now, isn't this romantic?" she said. He didn't want to laugh, but her humor was infectious.

"I would have laughed if you were a bit heavier than I thought, but I still won't drop you," he said.

"I appreciate the chivalry," she replied.

When he reached the bedroom, he was glad that the door was open. He entered, stopping briefly to kick the door shut.

He lay her on the bed when he reached it, loving the way she looked sprawled on his bed. There was a wanton vulnerability about her that excited him and his penis jerked with the knowledge that soon he'd bury himself inside her.

Gently, he helped her to take her dress off, all the while aware of the magic of her nakedness.

When she lay completely naked, he stood quietly devouring her luscious body, before he quickly took his clothes off and tossed them on the floor.

His penis, thick and straining for release, stood erect. For a brief moment, he felt embarrassed at his state, but then the pride he'd always felt at his generous size kicked in and he knew he would give her pleasure beyond anything she'd even imagined.

He lowered himself over her, careful not to put the full weight of his body directly on her, but she lifted her arms, placed them around him and drew him close.

"I want to feel you," she groaned as her body arched against him.

For a while he lay there, enjoying her softness, but then the need to pleasure her forced him to raise himself up.

Immediately he moved to her breasts. He had

to confess that he was a breast man, and a lovely pair like hers needed his undivided attention.

When he took the first nipple gently between his teeth, she moaned, arching her back toward him in surrender. He tugged tenderly on it, loving the way she begged him not to stop.

He started a sweet suckling, allowing his hand to move toward her vagina. When he slipped a finger inside her, her muscles contracted, exerting pressure on his hand, but he continued to work his magic, until she relaxed and allowed him further entry.

He reluctantly removed his finger—she was wet and ready—and focused on the next nipple before he placed his lips between her breasts, kissed the spot and then moved lower and lower until the hair around her vagina tickled him and he felt the urge to laugh.

When his tongue slipped between the delicate folds, her legs widened to give him entry. With his tongue, he soon found that special spot that would give her pleasure, and when he sucked it firmly, the sweet rush of her orgasm caused her to scream, and Russell knew he could wait no longer.

Her hands gripped his hair and he kissed the tender folds deeply before he moved upward.

She pulled him to her, holding him tight. "Make love to me," she said. "I want to feel you inside me."

Russell reached over her, opening the top drawer of the dresser, and pulled the new package of condoms out. Removing one, he took it from the package and rolled it slowly onto his erect penis.

Ready, he turned to her. Her eyes were closed, a picture of ecstasy.

When she opened her eyes he almost came undone. Russell saw a desire so raw and sensual he knew that what they would share would be special.

Positioning himself between her legs, he placed his penis close to her opening, teasing her with a back-and-forth movement that caused her to reach out and place her hand on his bottom, forcing him inside with a thrust that was hard and swift. The primal cry of mutual pleasure echoed in the silence of the room.

Her legs wrapped around him, giving him deeper entry, and when he started his slow, firm rhythm, she joined him.

There was something erotic about what was happening to him. When he caught a glimpse of them in the mirror, he knew that the image of them, shameless and wild, would fix itself in his mind for years.

And then Russell felt it—that slow building eruption of volcanic proportions. He felt it deep inside his gut, the heat and fire, until he felt that his body would catch on fire.

He could no longer contain himself. He wanted to tell her how he felt, about the magic she was working on him.

"Tori, you feel so good. I love being inside you. Move with me."

And soon she joined him with her own whispers of enjoyment and pleasure, until he finally reached the top and the power of his orgasm was so intense he heard his cry of release echo in the room. Seconds later, she joined him, her pleasure as intense as his.

His body jerked and his stomach contracted as each aftershock caused his body to convulse.

Russell held her close as her own body gave in to the wonder of what had just happened between them.

Exhausted, Russell moved to kiss her.

When he did, it was deep and filled with desperation.

"Thanks," she said. "You made me feel so alive. I haven't felt alive like this in years."

He turned onto his back, pulling her to him, her head against his chest. "It was incredible. We're going to have to do that again, but I think I'm going to fall asleep in a minute."

He closed his eyes, still aware of her softness against him.

During the night, Russell woke and automatically reached for Tori, only to realize she was gone.

In the silence he heard the steady patter of the shower and slipped from the bed.

When he entered the bathroom, her naked silhouette through the sheer curtain caused his erection to come hard and fast.

He wanted her again.

Pulling the curtain aside, he stepped inside the shower, feeling a sense of relief when she smiled and drew him to her.

Taking the soap she held, he created a lather before he soaped every inch of her body, his hands feeling the growing heat beneath them.

When he was done, Tori did the honors, her touch delicate but causing him to moan with excitement and anticipation.

He closed his eyes, only to feel her hand grip him and slowly begin to work its magic.

When he opened his eyes, all he could see was the top of her head as she prepared to take him in her mouth. For a while she pleasured him, her tongue taking him to a place of sensual excitement.

When she stopped, his penis stood erect and firm. He touched her, beckoning for her to stand.

Placing her back against the wall of the shower, the water cascading around them, Russell entered her for the second time that night, making love to her with a slow, leisurely pace.

With each stroke, he uttered her name, his excitement increasing the pace of his movement.

His climax, when it came, racked his body with pleasure and pain, and he almost collapsed to his knees. As his body shook, he felt her muscles around him contract. Tori's release took control of her body and she held on to him as if she would never let him go.

Later, after they'd showered, they lay in bed, both still awed by what had happened. His arms around her, Russell fell asleep, a smile of contentment on his face.

Chapter 3

Russell gathered his dreadlocks together, placing a rubber band around them. In the distance, the honking New York traffic welcomed the start of a new day. The single bird, perched on the window-sill, eyed him with a furtive glance.

Yawning, Russell stretched his arms. His body felt totally alive…as if every nerve ending had somehow become heightened in sensitivity.

Instinctively, he closed his eyes, inhaling deeply; forgetting that what he inhaled was the pollution of the city.

Though he loved the vibrancy of New York, he often ached for home. He loved the mornings; loved the quiet because it was in the stillness of the dawn that he made the journey back home to the sparking vitality of his island home.

In Barbados, on a morning like this, he'd be in his room, his hands urging the music from the steel pan he played with a reverence only a skilled player could understand. Tamara would start to accompany him with her sweet soprano and then Shayne would join in with his off-key tenor.

How much he missed the island!

But memories of home and those precious moments only brought sadness and pain. Russell knew that someday he'd have to return. In fact, after college several years ago, he should have returned to start work at a local newspaper; instead, he'd decided to remain in New York after a job was offered to him at the *Times*. He'd returned home briefly for Tamara's wedding, but the visit had not been a totally happy one.

Ironically, his brother, who'd been a source of inspiration, now threatened to stifle him. For years, his brother had taught them, he and Tamara, to listen to their own inner drummer, but yet wanted to force him back to the island.

Though Russell loved Shayne more than life itself, he didn't want to be at the mercy of his brother's need to keep them under control. Tamara called it love. Of course, Russell knew his brother loved him, but he also knew that he needed to grow; needed to be his own man before he returned.

Russell turned from the window and headed to

the bathroom, quickly taking a shower. He tried to ignore the lingering scent of the woman he'd made love to all night and into the early hours of the morning. The water cascading down his body did little to cool the fire that still raged inside.

Just as the sun was rising she'd awakened him, to tell him that she had to go. He'd taken his arms from around her reluctantly, only to be pulled closer as she kissed him.

Before he could seduce her back into his bed, she'd dressed quickly and rushed from the room, blowing a kiss at him.

Now everything in the apartment reminded him of her. He willed her naked image from his mind, but the task proved to be difficult.

He'd known many women, not that he'd been promiscuous, but none had stirred him like Tori Matthews. In this short space of time, she'd some-how ingrained herself within every fiber of his body. He didn't like it one bit. He was too accus-tomed to being in control, and the strangeness of his current vulnerability just didn't feel right.

He exited the shower, quickly donning his usual Levi's jeans, white shirt, tan jacket and a pair of Clarks that had seen better days.

Minutes later, he stepped out into the cool morning and crossed the street to get his usual breakfast from the coffee shop at the corner.

When he entered the shop, all eyes turned in his direction. He'd gotten accustomed to the stares, especially from the women. Women seemed to love him.

As he was leaving, his cell phone rang, and he flipped it open.

"It's Tori." Her voice caressed him with its soft huskiness. "I just called to make sure you were up. You did tell me you had an early meeting," she said.

"Yes, I'm up. Just walking out of the donut shop. I'll be on my way shortly," he replied.

"Then you have a nice day," she said.

"You, too. I'll call you later."

"Good, I wouldn't want it any other way."

"Tori," he said, before she could disconnect the call. "Want to take in a movie tonight?"

"I'd love to," she replied without hesitation. "I'm back at work tomorrow."

"Good, so I'll see you tonight," he said. "I'll pick you up. I'm sure I can find your apartment."

"Just call me on my mobile if you have any problems."

"I'm sure I'll be fine."

When the phone disconnected, Russell felt the unexpected urge to smile. Something was happening here that felt good.

Already, he wished it were night. He wanted to see her again. He wanted her. Last night had not been enough.

His hunger for her scared him. Tonight they'd have to establish clear ground rules. He didn't want anything to get in the way of his career plans, and he was sure she wanted the same. Tori's dreams for the future were too important to her.

He hoped this was just a question of lust. Maybe they'd hang together for a few months, work themselves out of each other's systems and then move on with their lives.

But a hollowness he'd never before experienced caused him to pause. Tori's effect on him was much greater than he had expected. He wanted to see her as just another woman in his life, but he didn't seem to be acting rationally these days.

Victoria was like no other woman he'd been with. And that scared him more than he was willing to admit.

He thought of his brother and sister. Each of them had fallen for the love bug and he had no intention of following his siblings into the confines of holy matrimony. Even the thought made him shiver.

He loved his freedom too much to give in to this gentler side of his personality, which kept whispering crazy stuff to him.

And it was crazy stuff.

Not now!

Not ever!

Tori slipped into the body-hugging blue blouse she'd splurged on and took a long look at herself in the mirror. She knew she looked her best, but

for the first time in a long while she took a good
critical look at herself.

She had no doubts about her assets, but though
she had smooth, unblemished, skin she often wondered if her lips were a bit too full for her narrow
face, or if her hips were a bit too generous.

She loved that her height—just an inch less
than six feet—allowed her to command attention
wherever she went. Most men found her intimidat-
ing, and maybe that accounted for the rare dates
she went on.

The phone rang, startling her. She answered.

"I'm near your apartment, but I can't find a
parking spot. What do I do?" he asked.

"I'll come downstairs," she said, immediately
reaching for her bag. "I forgot how difficult it is
getting parking around this time of day. I'll be
down in a bit."

"Okay, I'll be here."

Downstairs, Tori exited the building and looked
left and then right before she saw Russell waving
at her from a silver SUV. Tori turned and waved
goodbye to the doorman.

By the time she reached the car, Russell stood
on the passenger's side, his eyes following her
movement toward him.

Lord, he was fine!

She couldn't help but stare at him. Under the
streetlight she could see him clearly. He wore a
tam on his head and a white shirt that clung to his

body, emphasizing the well-defined muscles that rippled beneath.

"Like what you see?" he said, his voice sexy and filled with a touch of humor.

"I'm thinking about it. I've seen better, but you do have some potential," she retorted.

"Touché. It's good to know that you find me attractive. The feeling is definitely mutual."

"Now, aren't we being presumptuous?" she said.

"No, one doesn't have to be presumptuous when one can see the sizzle in the other person's eyes," he said, moving closer to her, until their bodies touched.

It was a sizzle she could feel at that very moment.

The honk of a car broke the moment and Russell pulled away. "Come, we have to go. The movie begins in half an hour."

The almost twenty-minute drive to the multiplex took place in silence, each of them enjoying the music, each of them acutely aware of the other's presence.

Bob Marley's "Redemption Song" pulsed from the high-quality stereo speakers. The fact that he loved good music was a plus in his favor.

Tori was content to listen to the music and speculate about the man next to her.

She was looking forward to the night, but if her heart didn't stop racing erratically, she was sure to end up in the hospital.

And she definitely couldn't let that happen.

She had every intention of waking up next to him in the morning.

In her bed or his?

It really didn't matter.

When they left the movie three hours later, Russell did all he could to calm the raging heat inside him.

In the cinema, Tori had reached for his hand, her touch sending jolts of white lightning through his body. Now, in the cool fall night, he felt a strange warmth inside.

When the evening had begun he'd wanted to take her back to his apartment and make love to her, but he felt different, weird, excited. Yes, he wanted her, but there was a part of him that wanted more. He wanted to get to know her, to fill in those blank spaces about her that had somehow become important to him.

The lovemaking their first time had been great. No, not simply great…earth-shattering, fabulous even. But he wanted to know the woman, the singer. He wanted to know all of her.

Who was she? What were her dreams? What made her smile? What made her…?

At a slight pressure on his hand, he turned to her.

She was looking at him, a concerned expression on her face.

"Is something wrong?" she asked.

"I'm sorry. Just something on my mind," he responded.

"Don't want to share?"

"Not yet, but I promise I will," he said.

"Don't want us keeping secrets from each other. I can't deal with secrets," Tori said. She stopped, and her look challenged him.

"I promise. No secrets," he replied.

"Good."

There was silence and it was as if time had stopped.

When his lips touched hers, he felt her body shudder, and she moved closer to him. Russell placed his arms around her in response, his body firm and hard, hers soft...so soft.

The kiss was more than a kiss; it was the touching of mind and spirit. Russell inhaled it, wanted it, needed it. He needed some affirmation that what existed between them was not mere feelings but a mingling of souls.

His tongue worked its magic, exploring, teasing, tasting, until he felt her tremble, her desire and excitement evident. Russell groaned when a wave of heat washed over his body.

A horn honked and the whistling from a vehicle passing by forced them apart.

Tori's face flushed with embarrassment, but he smiled down at her.

"I could kiss you all night," Russell commented, touching her cheek.

"I could let you kiss me all night," she responded. Her voice was husky with her desire.

Russell smiled. He enjoyed this verbal repartee between them.

"Don't tempt me, young lady," he said. "However, I have other plans for the night."

"Plans?" she asked, one delicate brow raised.

"Yes, so let's get in the car. I'm in the mood to make love to you, but before that we're going to do something fun." He knew he was being bold, but he wanted to be honest.

"Okay, I'm placing myself completely in your hands."

"Good," he said, taking her hand in his. "I like a woman who is willing to be adventurous."

Half an hour later, Tori's screams, mingled with those of twelve other thrill seekers, could be heard all across Coney Island beach. The Cyclone, the famous wooden roller coaster built in 1928, had been one of Russell's favorite rides when Shayne had brought him and Tamara the summer after their parents' death.

Now, though those memories surfaced, his focus remained on the fact that the ride would soon come to an end.

He'd been strong, holding Tamara while the ride made twist after painful twist. His stomach still felt like what he imagined the inside of a washing machine would feel. He'd been completely rinsed out.

Trying to walk steadily next to Tori, he realized how silly he was being.

"Tori, I won't ever be going on that ride again. I can't believe I loved that ride as a teenager."

"I know what you mean. Like you, that was my last one. Did you see that couple that went on again? They must be crazy. Just after coming off, they were back on."

For a while, they stood looking up at the ride, their breathing still heavy from the rush of adrenaline.

"You want to go stroll on the beach by the boardwalk?"

"Anything to take me far away from this killer ride."

Tori reached for his hand, drawing him to her side. She turned to him and smiled. "Thanks for bringing me here. With the exception of that thing they call the Absolute Thrill Ride, I enjoyed the others. You know what I'd eat right now? A hot dog from Nathan's with everything on it."

"You can eat at this moment? My stomach feels like it'll reject anything that comes near it. Let's walk first and I'll be sure to get you your hot dog later," he insisted.

"Okay, nothing troubles my stomach much. Don't worry, you'll be fine in a bit. You probably haven't done this recently."

"Definitely haven't, but I'm handling it. I'll be fine."

"Good, so I can go get my hot dog and we can walk," she emphasized.

"No problem, Tori. I'll get you two of the largest, most delicious hot dogs."

"Are you teasing me?" she asked.

"Of course not. Would I do that? I thought you knew me. I'm not the teasing kind," he replied.

"So you say. But I can hear the humor in your voice."

The sign announcing the historic Nathans hot dog beckoned them.

"I think I'm ready to have two of those hot dogs."

She laughed. "I knew you couldn't resist. I'll wait here."

While Russell ordered, Tori stood quietly, watching the array of people traveling back and forth, the diversity of characters passing.

As usual, the lines were long but the vendors worked quickly. As he approached, her heart surged and she noticed the smile on his face. He was happy. He wanted to be with her and the laughter within bubbled until she felt like running and hugging him.

On the beach, they sat on one of the benches on the boardwalk, savoring the hot dogs that somehow tasted special on occasions like this.

Across the bay, lights from passing boats flickered and he wondered if the people on board were as happy as he was. Being with Tori had changed his perspective on so many things. When he'd planned the day, he'd automatically thought of taking her to his home and making passionate love to her.

Tonight, things were different; the changes taking place in his psyche worried him. He was mellowing, but he wanted to hold on to that strong person whose heart beat inside him. He was beginning to feel schizophrenic. He laughed, watching as Tori turned to him, a puzzled look on her face.

The light from the moon caressed her, making her more beautiful than she already was. He inhaled deeply, wondering what it was about this woman that made his stomach tie up in knots.

Tamara, with her romance novels, would be the first to say that he was in love. But he didn't know. He thought he knew love. Each of the women he'd taken to bed, he'd loved in some way.

But what he felt now confused him.

Was this weakening of the knees each time he looked at Tori part of this strange thing called love?

He wasn't sure if he liked it one bit.

All he could think of at the moment was that he wanted to kiss her.

And kiss her he did. One of those sweet kisses that manifested itself in the gentle sound of music playing in his ears. This kiss was a mere touching of lips, a delicate whisper of nothingness, but yet he felt a part of this strange unexpected wonder that existed between the two of them.

Tori leaned toward him and placed her lips on his. This time the kiss lacked gentility, but demanded more from him. The sweetness still remained, but there was urgency in her ministrations.

Her hands reached down, cupping him, and caressed him gently until his erection strained against the confines of his jeans.

He couldn't take this much longer.

"I'm ready to leave," she finally whispered. "I want you to make love to me."

Russell didn't know how long it took him to get to his apartment, but he knew that he must have broken the speed limit to get there.

He didn't remember if there'd been any conversation between them. He did remember that Tori's hands had almost put him in a frenzy before he'd stopped her. He didn't want anything premature to happen.

Now, watching Tori lying naked next to him, Russell knew that this was the woman with whom he would spend the rest of his life.

He wanted to wake up each morning and find her just like this. Naked, vulnerable and totally his.

And he knew that she was his; knew it as he knew the sun would shine the next day.

He moved himself across her, his arms taking his weight for her whole body. He wanted to make this moment special, but there was a part of him that wanted to ride fast and wild.

"Russell, make love to me now. I can't wait."

His sentiments exactly.

He shifted slightly, spreading her legs and positioning himself between them.

When he entered her, the stroke took her by surprise. Hard and complete. Tori moaned her acceptance, wrapping her legs around him. He drew her even closer, burying himself deep within her until he became acutely aware of the soft contracting of her muscles around his penis.

With that, he started to move against her and in her, his strokes firm and hard. Tori, in turn, moved with him, her body joining him in a dance as passionate and hot as the salsa.

With each stroke, her muscles contracted around him, creating the sensual friction necessary.

When her body tensed, he did not hesitate. His own body ached for release and when it did come it was glorious, as glorious and vivid as a ray of sunshine after a storm.

When Tori eventually fell asleep, her body tired from the passion of their coupling, he continued to stare at her.

He loved this woman with an intensity that he hadn't known was possible, and still didn't understand.

He hadn't been looking for this, but love had crept up on him in the most unexpected way.

Tori Matthews felt something for him; he knew that much, but he couldn't—and wouldn't—settle for less than all of her.

He knew that Tori was her own woman and she

had dreams for her future, but would she put love before those dreams?

With that thought Russell fell asleep, stifling the urge to make love to her again.

The lovemaking would come in time. It was the love he was concerned about.

And for the first time in his life, Russell felt the need to be loved.

Chapter 4

When "The Call" finally came, Tori wasn't sure what to expect. All she did know was that when she put the phone down from talking to her agent, who had just spoken with the president of RIC Records, she couldn't say a word. She just sat there trying to absorb what he'd just told her.

Tears she couldn't control trickled down her cheeks, but she was determined to share her news. First she had to phone her mother.

Why was she calling? She didn't know but she needed to let her mother know that she'd finally made it. The news would make no difference to her father. She'd long accepted that he wanted nothing to do with her.

She realized the futility of it all and knew that some of the tears trickling down her cheeks were a result of the isolation she felt from her family.

She missed her brother, Jake. She'd begged him to come with her when she'd left, but he'd refused. He'd always been Daddy's boy and despite witnessing all that went on in the household, he'd refused to leave.

Of course, he was more likely studying to be a doctor as their father had planned. Tori refused to ask her mother for him and her mother never offered any information.

Maybe she could call Russell. He'd share in her joy.

Last night had surprised her. Their relationship had moved to another level. Despite the passion they'd felt for each other, he'd fallen asleep in her arms, and they didn't make love.

It was almost as if they'd taken a step backward and the passion burning between them had lowered itself to a flame that burned slowly instead of the sudden burst of passion that had taken over when they first met.

Her feelings for him worried her. She'd never felt like this about a man before. There was an overwhelming awareness of him every time he was near, and even when he was not, like now. He consumed her every thought until he was slowly becoming a part of her.

She picked up the phone, dialing the number

that had already become ingrained into her every-day existence.

He answered almost immediately.

"Hi," he said. "I wondered when you would call."

"I have some good news for you."

"What is it?" he asked.

"I received the call from the president of the record company a few minutes ago."

"So what did he say?"

"He's talking with my agent right now to discuss the details of the deal."

"Which company?" he asked.

"RIC Records," she replied.

"Wow, that's one of the major labels. You must be proud."

"Thank you. Do you want to come over tonight and help me celebrate?"

"I'm not doing anything tonight. What time?"

"Good. It has to be after work."

"I'll come by the club and pick you up after you're done," he said.

"I'll be there."

"See you."

When she heard the click of the phone, she held it close. Tonight would be special. She wanted to make love to him.

Against her better judgment, she dialed the other number.

She listened while it rang for almost a minute

before she decided to break the connection. Before she could hang up the phone, someone picked it up.

"What do you want?" her mother asked. "I told you not to call. I'll do all the calling."

She'd called at a bad time as usual.

"Mom, I just wanted to give you the good news. A record company wants to sign me."

"Your father is home. I can't talk long." For a moment, there was silence. "I'm glad for you. At least, you got to do what I wasn't able to."

"You won't leave him," Tori accused.

"Leave him and go where? Listen, I have to go. He's calling me."

"'Bye, Mom. Love you."

There was no reply, just the sharp dial tone that told her that her mother was gone.

Tori lowered herself to the couch and stared at the picture on the wall. She'd bought it a few years ago. She didn't know what had prompted her to buy it, but the artist had captured the essence of the island of Barbados. Alana Buchanan painted with a brush that seemed to make every splash of color come alive.

Ironically, Russell had told her he was from the island. To her, Barbados had always been a magical place, but out of her reach. Now the island was real and beautiful. She heard it in the nuances of Russell's speech whenever he talked about home.

Most of the time, the picture offered some sense of hope. Tonight, her thoughts troubled her as they did each time she spoke to her mother. She experienced a range of emotions that left her feeling tired and old.

Most of all she felt anger at a man who'd donated his sperm to give her life. She could not help but hate the man who was her father.

She'd tried on several occasions after she moved out to get her mother to come live with her, but the woman always refused, declaring that she would not break her vows.

As if her husband didn't break them every day.

She forced the image of her father from her mind. Her stomach churned and she inhaled deeply knowing that the feeling would pass.

She was glad Russell had come into her life at this moment. She needed someone to be there for her. And his interest in her made him the ideal candidate.

She stood. She didn't have to deal with this now. Tonight, she just wanted to be with someone who made her feel special. The first time her father had caught her singing a love song, he'd dealt with her harshly.

Tonight, she had every intention of making sure she was around when Russell arrived.

When Russell entered her apartment that night, it took all her willpower not to rip his clothes off and make love to him right there and then.

From the moment he arrived, the spark between them ignited the place.

He stepped into the room, liking what he saw. White and green decorated every corner of the house.

"You like green?" he teased, looking down at her.

"It's obvious, isn't it? I've been promising to add some brighter colors, but each time I do I change my mind," she replied.

"But I like it. It's bright, fresh, happy. I would love to live here," he said.

"I'm glad you like it. I've put a lot of work into what I'm doing to the house."

It must be a lot of money she was spending.

He wondered for the first time who her parents were.

In the short time they'd known each other she'd said very little about her parents. In fact she'd said nothing at all about them.

He followed her down a wide corridor and then stopped as she drew back the curtains that led to the room where the music was playing loudly. Bob Marley again. Good, cool, level vibes. Russell hoped she was not playing it just for him.

"You like Bob?" he asked her.

"Who doesn't?" She seemed surprised that he'd asked.

"Well, I know a few…"

"Yes, I'm just kidding. I'm sure that they're many who don't appreciate good classic reggae."

"But you do?" he asked.

"Definitely. My best friend in high school was

from Jamaica. We'd listened to all types of music, but her father was all into reggae. I don't hear from her too often, but we're still the best of friends. I just read in the newspaper that she'll be the lead in a new Broadway musical debuting this year."

"You must let me know when the show is out. My sister Tamara and I are big theater fans. Our brother used to let us come to New York almost every summer," he said.

"I've been a couple of times. Love the musicals, of course. I try to go at least twice a year."

"Now that we're on to music, would you like to dance?"

"I would love to."

She couldn't help it. She moved toward him, loving the feel of him as his arms came immediately around her.

Heaven.

He smelled good. One of those male scents that was woodsy and earthy at the same time.

For a while they danced to the music, their bodies moving with the sway and rhythm of the pulsing reggae beat.

She rested her head against his chest, feeling the steady beat of his heart. He pressed against her, and she moved even closer until their bodies were one.

Soon a heat flamed at the core of her womanhood and she tried her hardest to control her warring feelings.

Instinctively, her head tilted upward and she felt her body melt when his lips touched hers. She parted her lips, allowing him access. She loved the feel of his lips.

His mouth moved from hers, making its way along the curve of her neck until she felt her body shudder with the tingle that flashed along her spine.

Abruptly, he pulled away from her, moving across the room. She looked at him, questioning, wondering.

"I don't want to be held responsible for what will happen here tonight if I don't stop. I want to make love to you, and a part of me is definitely willing and ready, but I promised myself that tonight we'd be using this time to get to know each other."

Nodding, Tori indicated her agreement.

Inside, she felt unfulfilled and empty.

Russell didn't know what had gotten into him, but he seemed to be losing it. Another time and place a few months ago, he would have taken what she'd offered.

He looked at her, standing a mere arm's length away, and knew she was as aroused as he was.

He wanted her with a fever in his blood that was not reflected in the position he was currently taking. Tonight they would make love, but he didn't want it to be like this. He wanted to make it special.

He would wine her and dine her and then he'd make love to her until he felt he had enough of her.

"Come, let's eat. I'm starving." Though he was hungry, his hunger for Tori ran even deeper, so much so that the erection continued to throb inside his trousers. He was glad he'd worn something loose instead of the close-fitting jeans he usually liked to wear.

Hindsight stood him well. He didn't need to walk about with a telltale bulge before him.

"Dinner is ready, so we can definitely eat. I hope you like pasta," she said.

"Definitely. Of course there are few things I don't eat. I have a healthy and hearty appetite."

Her raised eyebrow told him she understood everything he said.

"Let's go eat," she said, indicating that he should follow.

"With pleasure," he replied.

He followed her out of the room, down the same corridor but in the opposite direction.

She turned left and they entered the dining room. On the table was food.

"You can sit. I just need to collect some things from the kitchen."

She disappeared out the door and he stood quietly for a while. The room was simply decorated, but like the others he'd seen, it radiated class.

Again he wondered who she was. She was definitely not a struggling singer. At a glance, he could tell that many of the things in the room bore designer labels. Definitely the genuine thing. He wondered if she was a kept woman, but rejected that thought immediately. No, he knew her well enough to know that she wouldn't let any man control or own her. She was too independent, too secure in who she was to need a man to take care of her.

He would gladly have offered to take that position a few months ago. Now he felt different and the change worried him. But tonight he didn't want to think of who he'd been or who he was. He just wanted to enjoy the company of a beautiful woman and then spend the rest of the night buried between her legs.

The distinct wisp of her fragrance forced him to turn around and he did, amazed at the impact she had on him.

She stopped abruptly as if aware of his thoughts. She looked at him, her head slightly tilted, her lips parted, and then she smiled.

"Dinner is served. I hope you're as hungry as you said."

"Oh, I assure you I'm famished." And he was. He'd not yet eaten today. The story he was working on had consumed all of his time. He waited until she took her seat before sitting next to her.

"You're working too hard, then," she said. "Never allow yourself to get too caught up in your work that you don't take care of yourself."

"You're beginning to sound like my brother, Shayne. He's a stickler for mealtime."

"Then I'd like to meet him. He and my mother could shake hands."

The way she said "mother" caused him to wonder, but he quickly put the thought from his mind. To ask about her family and friends at this time would be looking for trouble.

For now, he'd just sit here with her and enjoy the meal.

He had a strong feeling the dessert was going to be just as enjoyable.

An hour later, Tori watched as Russell put the spoon down and rubbed his stomach with a satisfied look on his face.

"I don't need to ask whether you enjoyed the meal or not. The expression on your face is one of utter contentment," she commented.

"You cook well," he said.

"Thanks to my mother and a British boarding school."

"Well, wherever your school was they taught you well. I can't tell Gladys that I found someone that cooks as well as she does."

"She seems important to you."

"Yes, she is," he replied. She heard genuine affection in his voice. "When our parents died when I was just twelve, Shayne was left to raise us, Tamara and me. Gladys stayed on and took care of us. Shayne would not have been able to do it if she hadn't been there. She's like a mother to me."

"So you have a brother?"

"Yes, and a twin sister, Tamara. She's a vet and married. She's pregnant with twins."

"She must be excited."

"Yes, she is. She did have a miscarriage a few years ago, so she has to be careful."

"Your brother is married, too?" she asked.

"Yes, and he has two children. Darius and Lynn-Marie."

"So you're the single one."

"Yes, and loving it. Won't change it for the world."

"So you have no intention of getting married?" she asked.

"I won't say 'no intention' but definitely not any time soon. I'm like you. Happy as I am. That's not to say I'm in any way promiscuous. I assure you, I'm not."

"You just enjoy the company of a beautiful woman?" she said.

"Yeah, I do. Not ashamed to say it, either. I'm the typical man. Warm-blooded and not ashamed to indulge in the occasional dalliance."

"I'm not sure I like being called the occasional dalliance."

He stood, moving closer to her. "I promise you, whatever happens between us, you're definitely not a dalliance."

"So what am I?" she purred. She could feel the warmth of his body behind her, the heat of his arousal.

"I know you're on my mind every waking moment. I don't know if I like it, but it seems I can't do anything about it. I've lost all control."

"I didn't think you ever lost control," she said, standing to face him.

"Until you, I didn't know it was possible. I've always prided myself on being in control. See, even admitting what you did to me is unlike me."

"Then maybe I should put all this to the test. There is something exciting about having someone like you doing my bidding," she teased.

"I can see you like playing games."

"Far from it, Russell. I'm definitely not playing games right now." With that she moved closer to him, her head tilted upward.

She wanted Russell Knight to see how much she wanted him.

He remained still, unmoving, as if he wanted to cherish the moment.

Tori couldn't wait, she placed her hand behind his neck and pulled his head down to her, anticipating the passion of his lips on hers.

When her lips touched his, Russell tried with all his discipline, but the groan of arousal had a mind of its own, and he opened his mouth, accepting her. In the basement of his mind, he acknowledged that he'd lost control.

She moved against him, her body fitting firmly in the curve, and he wondered how it was possible that a woman could be so perfect for him and yet so imperfect.

Her breasts pressed against him and he could not stop the hand that reached up and cupped the willing, firm orbs.

His other hand moved behind, skillfully lowering her zipper and exposing the soft curve of her shoulder.

He glanced down, feeling grateful that she wore no bra and that both breasts stood erect with their arousal.

He lowered his head, taking one nipple into his mouth, and wondered if honey could taste so sweet. She moaned, a barely audible purr, but one heated with her excitement.

For a while he suckled, loving the power of her response.

He moved to the other breast, offering the same care and attention. Her response intensified.

When her body began to shake and shudder with her release he felt a macho pride to know that he alone could move her to respond like this.

"Come, let me make love to you," she said, when her breathing had returned to its normal rhythm. "Let's go to the bedroom," she suggested.

"No, no bedroom. Here, I can't wait any longer."

And in a rustle of clothing and ripping buttons, he soon stood naked before her, feeling a moment of vulnerability.

Strange, since she'd seen him naked before. But Tori was different. She resurrected feelings he didn't think still existed. He'd long passed the love stage, but she made him feel special and he didn't feel that he deserved it.

When Russell slid inside her, smooth and firm, Tori groaned with pleasure. She'd reached a third, earth-shattering orgasm before he finally decided to have mercy. He'd pleasured her in a way that had left her aching for release.

No part of her body had remained untouched by his firm yet gentle hands. He'd caressed her and taken her to a place she'd never been before and still she wanted more of him.

Tori wrapped her legs around him, forcing him deeper inside her until she lost all sense of separation, but felt at one with him.

They danced the dance that had come down through history, but somehow the dance was different. It was their dance, a unique joining of souls that she'd never experienced before, and the thought scared her, but at the moment she was too immersed in the pleasure that he gave her.

With each slow, leisurely stroke, he felt as if he'd found another part of her, of who she was, and the body he dwelled in would never be the same.

Soon, Russell felt that familiar awakening, the

shiver of excitement, the tensing of muscles and the tightening of mind.

When the explosion came, he closed his eyes, wanting to experience the kaleidoscope of colors that sparkled in his head.

Later that night, they made love again. This time their coming together was something unique. Tori knew that somehow she'd always remember this night.

Reentering the bedroom, she closed the door behind her, finding him already lying naked on the bed. He'd refused to put clothes on.

The sight of his manhood, standing firm and erect, excited her, but she wanted this time to be special so she tempered the urge to pounce on him and give in to her passion.

Instead she lowered herself to the bed, taking him in her hands and watching his body jerk with the anticipation.

She'd had a few lovers before, but none had moved her as much as this man who reminded her of the ocean and the windswept island he called home.

She bent her head, wanting to kiss him, and when her lips touched his, she groaned against him, loving the taste and feel of him.

Russell came slowly awake, immediately aware of the sleeping woman next to him.

He loved her…or at least he thought he did. Russell wasn't sure what love was, but if this overwhelming need he felt had anything to do with it, then he wasn't far from being in love.

There was just something special about Tori.

Being around her made him feel weak and vulnerable, but he also felt strong and confident. He wanted to protect her, to be there for her, to be her all.

At times, he imagined her lying next to him, her stomach swollen with child—his child—and knew that he wanted that more than anything.

For years, his ideal woman had been this beautiful outdoor woman, who didn't care much about makeup and dressing up. Tori was far from that image. Yes, she was beautiful, but he could tell she was born to wear designer dresses and expensive fragrances. Even when she wore jeans and T-shirts she wore them with a sophistication and elegance that came from a cultured background.

He wondered about her family, her parents. She didn't talk about them at all.

There were so many things about her he wanted to know, but for now he'd have to be content with what she was willing to give.

But he wanted so much more.

Shayne closed the door behind him. He moved immediately to the chair that had become his refuge at night. He loved his wife and his son, but sometimes he needed to be on his own. Just for five minutes or so, he needed to be alone.

His gaze shifted instinctively to the picture that hung above the shelf brimming with books his wife never seemed to tire of adding to. Of course, he taught her that she didn't need any romance novels, since he provided all the loving and romance she needed, but to no avail. At least the books were one shared interest of his wife and his sister, Tamara.

His gaze moved to the boy he called his brother. To say he was disappointed with his brother was an understatement. He'd had so many plans for Russell. He'd thought his brother had so much potential. He was sure he'd be the doctor he always dreamt his brother would be. However, when Russell had informed him he wanted to study journalism, he'd cringed, but controlled himself enough to offer his support. He'd always taught them to follow the beat of their own drum, so he'd had no choice but to support Russell.

Shayne had to admit that the choice Russell made had proven to be a good one. He now worked at one of the leading newspapers in the U.S.

But his brother was not here in Barbados. He missed him more than he could imagine.

He could forgive Russell his locks, he could even forgive him not studying in the West Indies, but his brother hadn't been home since Tamara's wedding almost three years ago.

It hurt.

Yes, there was the occasional e-mail and the rare phone call.

But he wanted more.

Shayne heard the scramble of footsteps along the corridor and then Darius raced into the room. Shayne glanced at his son. Now five years old, Darius was the apple of his eye. He loved Lynn-Marie, but he knew the bond that existed between he and his firstborn would be a special one.

He remembered how he'd met Carla again after their initial tryst and discovered she was pregnant. He'd not wanted a child and then he'd seen his son and he'd fallen hopelessly in love with his fragile offspring. Each night, he never failed to thank God for giving his son the strength to live. When he looked at Darius he could not believe that the strong, strapping youngster was the same underweight bundle he'd held in the palm of his hand.

He reached for the phone. He needed to hear his brother. He dialed the long distance number and listened as the phone rang.

Russell's voice came over the distance, strange and mature.

He put the phone down, not leaving a message. His brother was probably entertaining one of the long line of females who kept him busy. Tamara had kept him informed of his brother's playboy lifestyle.

Russell was his own man; all he hoped was that his brother took care of himself and would some-day find love.

Chapter 5

A part of her wondered how he'd accept the fact that she needed to focus on her new life, that their relationship had to be put on hold. Her meeting with the president of the record company was just a week away and she needed to be focused. Russell didn't allow her to be focused.

Things between them had begun to change or had changed. Russell wanted more. He hadn't said it, but he told her in the way he looked at her with those bedroom eyes that caressed her with every glance. He told her each time they lay in bed after making love all night, and he held her in his arms and whispered sweet nothings to her.

She'd wanted the music for so long, but she'd

never questioned the value of it until Russell came into her life and started to work his way into her heart.

Tori had never wondered if a life of music in the public's eye was the right thing for her. She'd always been willing to give up everything to sing. Now she knew she wouldn't have time for both. She'd seen enough of the world of the music industry to see that not many marriages lasted.

But what was she doing talking about marriage?

Who said anything about marriage?

Russell didn't seem like the marrying type. Tori had learned enough about him from Rachel to know his reputation. Yeah, she knew that sometimes reputations were blown out of proportion, but she also knew that there was a little bit of truth in what she'd learned.

Russell Knight loved women.

She saw it in the way he walked, the way he loved and the way he made love, and she was his latest conquest.

Tori had no intention of being like her mother. She knew where her talent had come from. Marilyn Matthews had been one of the best singers on Broadway, and then she'd married Tori's father, Benjamin Matthews. Merry, as she was known then had given up her dream for the man she loved; only to find herself victim of a marriage that had psychologically damaged her. Her only wish in life had been to serve the man who owned her.

Tori had made sure she got out. Her father had refused to let her sing. So she'd hidden and taken classes after school with Ms. Gilmore, claiming to be in the chemistry club.

The day she turned eighteen, she packed her bags and—with the money she'd been saving for years—moved to New York. She'd refused to look back and only found the courage to pick up and call her mother after a few years. When a trust fund legally became hers on her twenty-first birthday, she immediately quit her job and made plans to enter college.

Ironically, she had planned her life down to the most precise detail. Despite her desire for a singing career, she'd earned her undergraduate degree in music to ensure she had something to fall back on if her planned singing career didn't succeed. And of course, despite her father's attempt to stop her from getting her trust fund, she was now a comfortable woman.

But she'd never been one to do nothing, and her job at the club, though a way of getting known, was something she enjoyed doing.

In fact, her stint at the club had brought her to the notice of the president of RIC Records. When Dane Collins had requested a demo, she'd been elated, and thanks to her contacts from college, she'd made a demo that was professional and demonstrated the wide range of her vocals and her writing.

Now here she was floundering about something she had wanted for so long, because of a man who made her heart race, and made her think of the pitter-patter of babies' feet and happily-ever-after.

She needed to think this situation through. Maybe when the time came to discuss their future, she and Russell could come to some workable compromise.

But the different scenarios playing out in Tori's mind didn't ease the sense of dread she was feeling.

She picked the phone up and quickly put it down.

She definitely wasn't ready to talk to her mother.

Russell picked the phone up for the umpteenth time that morning and put it down again. He was definitely not acting like a man who devoured women with the snap of his fingers. He was acting like a randy teenager with a crush who was unsure of how to talk to the pretty girl in his class.

He was going away on assignment to Dallas for a few days and wanted to talk to Tori before he left. He knew to call her would suggest something, but he didn't really care.

Inhaling deeply, Russell dialed again, this time allowing it to ring. When Tori answered, her voice warm and friendly, he could not remember what he wanted to say.

"Hello," she repeated, this time her tone seeming impatient.

"Hi, Tori, it's Russell."

"Russell, I was about to put the phone down. Thought it was another wrong number. I've had several for the day."

"Sorry, didn't mean to alarm you," he said.

"No problem. I'm just here reading a book. Nothing else to do until I go to work tonight."

"I just called to let you know I will be away for the weekend. The newspaper is sending me to Dallas to cover a conference there at the Hyatt. I was hoping I could see you this weekend, but I only found out when I went into work this morning."

"Oh, I would have liked that," she replied. The disappointment in her voice pleased him. "But I hope you have a good time."

"I'm not sure if I could say I'll have a good time since I'll be working," he said, "but I promise I'll miss you."

Tori remained silent. He knew she'd not expected his words. Truth be told, he hadn't expected to say it, either.

"I'll miss you, too." Her voice was low. "I have something to talk to you about when you return," she said.

"You're sure it can wait?"

"Yes, I want to tell you in person, so yes, it can wait."

"Good…we will talk as soon as I return," he said. "Well, I have to go now. Have to go talk with my senior editor and then head on home, get my suitcase and I'm off. I'll call you tonight?"

"Remember, I'll be at work until one a.m."

"Sorry, maybe I'll call in the afternoon when you're up."

"No, you can call tonight if you want. I'll be home by one-thirty."

"Good, I'll call. 'Bye."

"'Bye," she replied.

Russell realized the extent of his feelings for Tori when he entered his hotel room that night. He closed the door, glancing around at the classy decor, but it failed to give him comfort.

He pulled his shirt over his head and stepped out of the jeans he'd worn all day. He'd enjoyed butting heads with the senator he'd interviewed. He loved his work, and the accomplishment he felt at the end of each assignment stroked his ego. He knew he was good at his job, and with each assignment he knew his boss saw him more as an asset to the newspaper. Not that by any means was he irreplaceable, but Russell knew he was doing a good job.

But each night he came home to an empty apartment. He wasn't even sure if he considered the apartment home. If he were honest with himself, he would admit that he missed the island, and tonight, like each night, the scent of a warm tropical breeze wafted through the air almost as if he were there.

He knew he would have to deal with Shayne sooner than later. He wanted to go home, wanted to be around his family, wanted to see his nephew and niece—Darius and Lynn-Marie—and his sister.

He missed his uncles, Troy and George. They were not his real uncles, but his father's best friends from high school. He never ceased to be amazed at how close they were. Sadly, he didn't have any friends like that. At school, he'd been the nerdy type, immersed in his books and music and nothing else.

New York had changed him. He'd decided to use the gym on campus, slowly buffing up, and then the girls had started coming on to him.

The first time he'd made love to a woman at twenty-one, he'd come down from his first experience wondering what he had been doing to miss out on a delight so decadent.

After that there had been no stopping him. He'd made up for the years of self-imposed virginity. The women came and went and he had enjoyed each delectable body with the same intensity he'd given to his school work.

He'd immediately made up his mind that he wouldn't allow his newfound pastime to interfere with his studies. His school work had not suffered. In fact, with his transformation from nerd to hunk and his reputation for being super intelligent, he'd had no lack of women.

But he had no friends.

Though he and Tori were only friends, he felt a spark of something else beyond the desire to strip her clothes off each time he saw her.

He loved the way she laughed and her quick wit.

Russell glanced at the clock. 11:45 p.m. still a

long way to go before she left work. He needed to get out of the hotel room before he went crazy.

He'd take a shower and then head on downstairs to the restaurant on the outside. He preferred the noise of the locals to the starched staidness of the business people who frequented the hotels at this time.

His mind made up, he scampered into the shower and quickly erased the tiredness of his long day's work, before he stepped into a pair of black slacks and a close-fitting black polo shirt.

He glanced at the mirror nonchalantly. He knew he looked good; knew that if he wanted a companion for the night, it'd be a simple matter of cocking his finger and she'd follow.

Ten minutes later, he sat lazing in the coziness of the restaurant. Already, a cute thirty-something woman had dropped by to chat with him. She'd pretended to be all business, but the way she subtly touched his hands made her intention quite clear.

Russell wondered what she'd do if he took her to his room and made love to her all night.

But he couldn't.

A very bold image in his mind surfaced. He was losing his touch. He'd always been a master of his own fate. Now Tori Matthews had, in a very short time, taken a bit of that away.

Two more days and he'd be able to go back home. Home?

Back to another night of loneliness.

But back to Tori's arms, he hoped.

Tori had given him back the gift of sleep. The two occasions he'd fallen asleep in her arms, he had slept like a baby, something he'd not done in years.

He was the perfect night owl. Did most of his work at night, and often with nothing to do, he'd turn to Turner Classic Movies and watch old films he'd never seen into the early morning until, exhausted, he'd fall into a restless sleep.

Dinner completed, he was on his way back to the hotel when he noticed the flashing neon light of a club. He loved to dance. The spirit of his ancestors touched him with their rhythm.

He smiled, remembering the few occasions he'd been out to parties with Tamara. On those outings he'd enjoyed himself, loving the easy way with which his body moved to the music.

In the club, he headed immediately for the bar, ordering soda water. He didn't make it a habit to drink—he'd come to enjoy the music.

On the dance floor, the dancers moved to the music of the latest hip-hop, pop and R&B. He watched, appreciating their ability to just enjoy themselves. He couldn't remember the last time he'd done something so spontaneous; even when he'd gone to Tori's club, he'd been invited by its owner, Rachel.

At his side, a woman cleared her throat and he turned around. A prettily made-up face didn't fail to hide her natural beauty. He looked her up and down. She was a bit older than his usual type, but he liked what he saw.

"So you're going to buy a drink for me?" she asked.

"What are you drinking?" Russell responded.

"I'll drink a margarita. The next drink is on me, if you don't mind. Don't believe much in this macho stuff that you men believe in."

"Fair enough," Russell replied. She had a sense of humor. He liked that in a woman.

"So, what's a sexy young brotha like you doing in here all by yourself?"

"Nothing much. Just enjoying the music."

"You here on your own?"

"Yes, I'm here for a conference at the Hyatt. Just didn't want to stay in the hotel all night."

"So you don't mind the company?" she asked.

"No, but just the company, nothing else."

"Oh, you have a girl back home?"

"You could say so."

"Oh, having some hard times?"

"In a manner of speaking. But we're working things out. But I'm sure you don't want to stand here and chat about my love life."

"Oh, I'm fine with anything you want to talk about. I'm staying at the Hyatt, too. Covering a story there."

"Are you a journalist?" Russell asked.

"Yes, with *Entertainment Weekly*."

"Interesting? I work for the *Times*."

"That's interesting. I worked there a few years ago, but I wanted to spend a bit more time with my husband. Little did that help. He'd already found himself a girlfriend half our age, and I found myself a single mother in the process."

"He couldn't handle your schedule?" Russell asked.

"No, he couldn't," she replied, "but that was only a part of the problem. I'm sure we could have worked it out if he'd wanted to."

"Girl, I feel your pain."

"Oh, you're dealing with issues, too," she commented.

"Yeah, I think I'm falling for her. Hard."

"And you call that an issue?"

"Yeah, I don't think either of us wanted to get married. Or should I say, we'd agree to enjoy ourselves with each other, but nothing more," he said.

"Oh, and I can guess that you're falling for her badly and now want more."

"You shouldn't be a journalist. You were born to be a psychologist."

"Oh, that was the plan at one time. I'm sure my husband would have loved that. Instead, I went into journalism just to piss him off. He wanted me to do something a bit more reputable. I eventually did. Our marriage got its share of write-ups in the news and tabloids."

"So you're someone famous," he said.

"*Notorious* may be the better word. The press didn't place me in a good light. Not if your husband is one of the country's most prominent heart surgeons."

"Oh, but you're moving on with your life?" he asked.

"I am. Finally got up the courage to paint the town and I end up with a man who's in love with someone else."

"That doesn't mean we can't be friends. I'm Russell Knight."

"And I'm Linda. Linda Cole."

"You're Linda Cole. You're legendary. We studied your work in college."

"Oh, you're making me blush."

"Sorry, didn't mean to embarrass you."

"That's fine. And from a man with a Caribbean accent. Let's see, I used to be good with these accents. Definitely not Jamaican and I do hear a bit of the proper British accent, so I'd say Barbados, and final answer."

Russell laughed. "I confess I'm a Bajan."

"So, what are you doing here when you could be back on the island with its white sands and beautiful beaches? I was there a few years ago."

"Oh, I've been thinking about that lately. My studying is over and going back home may be the best thing."

"I can tell that's one of the problems that has reared itself."

"Yes, but as you've said I'll deal with it day by day."

"Yeah," she replied. "You wanna dance?"

"I wondered when you were going to ask. Didn't want to put the macho thing on you and yes, I'd love to dance."

"Yes, it'll be no problem. That's why we are friends."

Tori sipped the glass of wine Taylor Carrington had poured for her. Her agent sat across from her. In the distance she could hear their voices, but nothing registered.

The most important event in her life and all she could think of was Russell. She shook her head trying to focus on the discussion between her agent and her new boss. The initial discussion had served to prepare her for what was to come.

In a few days she'd be going into the studio to do a demo recording and then selections of additional songs for her album. Two of the songs she'd written had been accepted.

"Well, young lady. I feel honored to officially welcome you to RIC Records. I have no doubt that in time, as soon as the first album is out, you'll have everyone eating out of your hand. Of course, I don't mean literally, but you know…I don't think I've been as excited about a singer as I am about you."

"I have every intention of giving my best."

"Your reputation follows you. Your boss at the

nightclub is proud of you. Unfortunately, you won't be able to sing there any time soon."

"I just want one request…that one of my official launches takes place there. The mileage would be good for Rachel. She gave me a chance to sing when I needed one."

"Oh, I have no doubt that you'd make it, but I understand what you mean. I'll see that the request is put into writing."

"Thank you," she responded.

"Well, that's good. I'll see you at work on Monday."

"I'll be here."

Tori stood, shaking his hand before she left.

When Tori closed the door behind her, she headed straight for the elevator. She pressed the button and waited.

Inside, she leaned back, resting against the wall's coolness.

It was only then that she allowed the tears of joy to trickle down her cheeks.

She'd finally achieved her dream…or at least she was on her way there. Life was really funny. She'd finally achieved what she had wanted out of life. She knew that there would be hard work ahead. The thought that she would not succeed did not even enter her mind. She'd long planned this, long worked this day out in her mind, but she had never expected to be in a situation like this. Her dream in her grasp, she'd never expected that a man would make this moment lose so much of the joy it promised.

She remembered that her new boss had told her life was no longer her own and she had to give herself completely over to her music.

So why wasn't she feeling the intense joy she had expected? The reason lay in the connection she'd shared with Russell.

Was she willing to lose her dreams?

Or was love more important?

The night Russell returned from Dallas, Tori sat at the piano tinkering with a song she was working on, but she couldn't concentrate.

When the phone rang, she rushed over to it and was disappointed when she discovered that the caller had dialed the wrong number.

Frustrated, Tori placed the phone in its cradle and was about to head out to the nearby supermarket when the doorbell rang.

When she looked through the peephole, Russell stood there, a broad smile on his face.

She opened the door quickly, feeling complete when he automatically wrapped his arms around her, his lips finding hers.

Russell kicked the door shut and proceeded to show Tori how much he missed her.

Tori gave herself totally over to the fires raging inside. She didn't want to hold back anything, so she gave herself to him freely, body and mind.

The kiss ended as quickly as it had begun, but only to allow them to get to the bedroom.

Tori trembled in anticipation, knowing that soon they would be making love.

She wanted to make love, needed confirmation of his need for her. Tori felt his responding shudder and raised her head to look at him. When his lips lowered to hers again, she groaned with the sweetness of the pleasure she felt.

Russell pressed himself firm and hard against her and she loved the feeling.

She felt his hand at her back, releasing the buttons of the blouse she wore. The coolness of the silk against her skin caused her to shiver. He kissed her shoulder softly and made his way along her neck, where he nibbled tenderly, the heat inside making her wonder if she would catch on fire and combust right there.

His lips continued their journey, his tongue toying briefly with one breast, then the other, and then back to her lips.

He kissed her deeply, and she willingly responded to his urging, her own tongue tangling with his as she tasted the sweet honey he offered.

While they kissed, her blouse fell to the floor, exposing her breasts to his gaze. She stood wantonly, unconcerned at the sight she must make. Tonight, there was no time for hang-ups. She just wanted to give herself to him. She didn't want to think of for-

ever; there were never any guarantees in life, but tonight she wanted him.

Russell stared at her, his gaze burning her with its heat and desire.

And then he lifted her, not moving until she was comfortable, with one arm around his shoulder.

He moved quickly and with purpose. His need for her was strong, and she could feel it in the tension in his body.

When they reached her bedroom, Russell pushed the door open with his body and entered, flicking the light on.

Tori welcomed the light. She wanted to see him when they made love.

He placed her gently on the bed and she lay there, her legs slightly apart, as he quickly stripped and discarded his clothes on the floor.

She'd seen him naked before, but she'd never really looked at him, and now she realized how beautiful the male form was, how beautiful *he* was.

Russell stood before her, allowing her to feast on him.

Tori sat up and reached for his manhood, feeling an unexpected surge of power when it contracted and jerked in her hands.

She leaned forward, taking him into her mouth. He was big, but the length of him felt total and right. Russell groaned his pleasure, and placed his hands on her head, guiding himself in and out with the slight movement of his hips.

Russell withdrew and beckoned for her to lie on the bed. She complied. She wanted to feel him inside her.

When he moved to take a condom from his pants pocket, she wanted to protest, but she realized that even in the midst of passion, he was doing the responsible thing.

His task completed, Russell reached for her and shifted her, placing a pillow under her buttocks. He climbed onto the bed, positioning himself between her legs.

Tori raised her lower body upward, aching for him, but he seemed to want to use the moment to tease her, the thick head of his manhood probing at her entrance.

Despite the foreplay, the force of his entry surprised her and she heard her cry of welcome echo in the room.

When Russell started to move, she could not contain herself. She urged him on with words that only served to make him increase the speed of his movement.

Inside she felt a flame spark and the heat slowly spread, causing her to move with a frenzied grind against him.

When he reached for her legs and placed them around his waist, she obeyed, knowing that the position would only give more pleasure.

With each stroke, she moaned, reveling in his own guttural response.

And then she felt it, the beginning of the end, that telltale stoking in her gut and the almost excruciating pleasure that caused the walls of her womanhood to contract, clenching him with each stroke.

She could tell he was near. His pace had slowed, was less controlled, but she could still feel every thick, long inch of him.

The intensity of her release, when it came, forced every muscle in her body to respond and a sweet relief washed over her when she gave in to the pleasure.

And then he followed her into that ultimate erotic experience with a raw cry that tore from within him, just before he captured her lips and tasted of her essence. His body contracted as spasm after spasm rocked him.

As their bodies cooled and calmed, he drew her close, hugging her tightly, her back against his chest.

Exhausted, Tori fell into a sweet, contented sleep.

When Russell awoke, Tori no longer lay next to him and he immediately panicked.

But the comforting scent of coffee was enough to drag him from the bed.

His stomach grumbling, he quickly took a shower, dressed in jeans and a T-shirt and headed to the kitchen.

Tori turned when she heard his footsteps. She wore one of his T-shirts, which reached just to the curve of her behind, but revealed her shapely legs.

He willed himself under control and felt proud when his body relaxed.

There would be time to make love to her again. He meant to hang around, so there was no need to go all sex crazy.

"Coffee is in the percolator over there and since you're here you're responsible for the toast. I'm making omelettes. My specialty. I've been told I make great omelettes."

He felt a flash of jealousy. He wondered whom she had over for breakfast often enough to enjoy her omelettes.

"Rachel sleeps over when we have a girls' night," she explained, as if expecting him to react that way.

His gaze met hers. The flicker of laughter he saw made him feel silly. He smiled in response.

"It's fine. We're just getting to know each other. But I promise you, there is no sordid past or any crazy ex-boyfriends hanging around in the wings."

"I'm sorry," he said and she nodded in acknowledgment.

"The omelettes are done and you've still not done the toast, Mr. Knight. I'll set the table while you do it," she said cheerfully. His indiscretion appeared forgotten. "The bread's over there." She indicated the counter.

Calmly he proceeded to do her bidding, aware of the cozy domestic picture they made. The jewelry box he'd placed in his pocket felt heavier than it actually was, and he wondered if he was doing the right thing.

He'd never done this before, but it felt right.

He placed the toast on two plates and moved to the table where Tori already sat.

When he joined her, she scooped an omelette with sweet peppers and onions onto his plate, and then one onto hers. He waited until she'd completed her own task before he started to eat.

Sitting with Tori like this, eating breakfast across from him, Russell felt warm and cozy.

An image of a little boy and girl sitting with them came vivid and clear.

He was going crazy, beginning to hallucinate.

When Russell laughed out loud, Tori turned toward him, a confused look on her face.

"You all right?" she asked.

"Oh, I'm fine. Couldn't be better," he replied.

"Okay, I'll take your word for it. It does, however, seem a little bit crazy when you laugh out loud for no reason."

Russell laughed again. It didn't matter what she thought.

He just knew that he felt happy, completely happy.

Chapter 6

The ring in Russell's pocket felt warm, almost alive beneath his touch. Tonight he had all intentions of proposing. He'd tried several times during the past week, but each time, he'd hesitated, wondering if he were making the right decision.

Tori seemed somewhat distracted, but she claimed that things were fine. Yet he felt the change even when they made love. She was holding back—something she'd never done since they became lovers.

Maybe the intensity of their relationship overwhelmed her as much as it overwhelmed him. Or maybe, as she'd said, nothing was wrong.

Tonight, however, he had all intentions of making things right. He was scared. He'd spent too much of his life enjoying his singlehood to give it up so easily. But he loved Tori; loved her with every fiber of his body.

Today had been perfect. His boss had complimented him on his recent feature and then topped it by offering him a raise—a generous raise.

Russell slipped out of the clothes he had worn all day, headed to the shower and completed the task in record time. He dressed quickly and took the shortest route to Tori's apartment.

When he arrived, the concierge let him in and he took the stairs, two at a time, to the third floor.

There he knocked, startled when the door opened immediately.

Tori smiled at him, reaching up to kiss him. His lips tingled at her touch.

She reached for his hand, leading him along the corridor and into the room she used to entertain guests.

Russell wondered if she'd guessed that this would be a special occasion. He wanted to ask her first before they ended up in bed together.

He didn't want her decision to be a result of the throes of passion. He wanted her to say yes because she loved him. He wanted what Shayne had found with Carla and Tamara with Kyle.

He wanted her love more than life itself.

On the table, dinner lay waiting, and when Tori indicated a seat, he obliged.

Hungry, Russell didn't waste time, digging in to

the succulent barbecue ribs and fluffy vegetable rice Tori had prepared.

An hour later they sat in the sitting room, sipping their umpteenth glass of wine and laughing at the sitcom *Everybody Hates Chris*.

Russell reached for the ring in his pocket, its warmth startling him. He must be hallucinating, but it seemed alive.

"Tori," he said quietly.

She turned to him.

He felt a bit awkward. He'd never done this before. And then he laughed.

"Listen, I really don't know what I have to say here." His heart was beating faster than usual. "I love you, Tori. More than I ever thought possible. This may not be the most romantic place to do this, but I'd be honored if you'd be my wife."

Her response, when it came, didn't shock him. All he felt was an overwhelming sense of loss and sadness.

"Russell, I'm sorry." He heard her voice somewhere in the back of his mind. "I'm not ready for marriage," she said. She stopped, as if unsure of her words. "You knew that. We talked about it."

He didn't know what to say.

"I thought things had changed…that we cared about each other."

"I care about you, Russell. You know I do. But…"

"But what?" he asked. Again she hesitated, and he knew something was definitely wrong.

He watched as two of her fingers tapped nervously on the rim of her glass.

"What?" he snapped.

"The record company called," she finally replied. "They offered me a deal."

"Called?" Curiosity got the better of him.

"A few days ago wh-while you were in Dallas," she stuttered.

"And you're just now telling me?" He couldn't believe she hadn't told him.

"I'm sorry. I wanted to tell you before."

"So you kept the truth from me? You lied." He tried to control his tone. He didn't want to shout, but the ogre inside him seemed to be slowly rising.

He stood, his body numb, but somehow he was able to take control.

"I think it's best if I leave now. We can talk about this later."

She didn't reply and he looked at her, not recognizing the woman who sat opposite him. Already she seemed different, colder.

He smiled, trying to maintain his composure. And then he turned, refusing to say anything else.

He needed to go.

He didn't want her to see the dampness of his eyes.

When he exited the apartment, he closed the door gently behind him.

Ironic…since all he wanted to do was slam the door shut, for dramatic effect.

* * *

Russell slammed the door behind him. He'd had enough of the fawning and pawing from the women in the club. He realized that coming here had done nothing for him.

In the past, he would have left the club with a voluptuous woman in tow and spent most of the night enjoying the decadence she offered.

Tonight, something was definitely wrong with him. Were his playboy days over?

No.

He had no intention of letting it happen. He'd learned a lesson.

Tori Matthews could take her record deal and stuff it….

What was happening to him?

Shame washed over him. He could not believe that he was acting like a spoiled child who couldn't get his own way.

He had to put this situation in perspective. He needed to deal with his feelings for Tori once and for all. This on-again, off-again personality was something that he did not wish to cultivate. Until he got things under control, he could not go on with his life.

Ironically, he'd been the one to emphasize the rules when the topic had come up. And now he seemed to be the one wanting to break them.

The best way to handle the situation would be to work his magic on her. Why fight her? Why not give her what she wanted? She wanted them to be friends; then friendship would be what she'd get.

And in the meantime, he'd work his magic on her. Oh, he knew she wanted him. He saw it in the tensing of her body and the flames that ignited in her eyes each time they were near.

Yes, this was going to be fun.

He was going to make Tori sing a love song for him straight to the altar.

And there was no better time than tonight.

He'd stop on the way over to her home. Pizza with pineapple, onions and pepperoni—her favorite.

He smiled, a slow leisurely smile.

Let the magic begin!

When he arrived at her apartment later that day, he knocked, his mood lightened, but his body tense.

The door opened slowly. She was not smiling.

"What are you doing here?" Tori was definitely not happy.

He moved the hand blocking his entrance and slipped inside before she could protest.

"A peace offering." He handed her the boxes. "I would have brought flowers, but I know you can't resist—"

"Pineapple, onions and pepperoni," she finished for him. She smiled.

"Yeah, exactly how you like it. And I remembered that you don't like extra cheese."

"But you like the extra cheese," she said.

"And that's why there are two boxes. One for me, one for you."

From the look Tori gave him, Russell could tell she knew she was melting.

"Is that what this is about, Russell? You coming to apologize and tell me you're willing to let me do what I want to do?"

He stopped in his tracks, the embarrassment heating his face. She was right. He'd come here to work his magic and already it seemed to be backfiring. "Okay, I confess. I want us to deal with this. I know you want your music. I know you want me as much as I want you. Maybe I started to think about it more. Maybe. But your music is important to you and if that means there is no time for a relationship right now, then I can live with it."

"But you're suggesting that we can have this relationship because you want it. It's not about you and maybe it's not about you and me, either."

"I didn't say that," he retorted. *Why do women always have to turn your words around?*

"But I'm saying it. This relationship can't work, Russell. You may *allow* me to go off and do my thing, but in a few months you'll be wondering why I'm never at home or asking yourself why I have to spend so much time in the studio. And to be honest, I can't deal with that right now."

"So does this mean what I think it means?" he asked.

"I'm really not sure what you want it to mean. I

do know that I have no intention of being like my mother. Tied to a man who controls her. I've worked hard to get where I am and I'm not allowing a man who only thinks about himself to take over."

In his head, he felt the slap across his face, but it never came.

The evening sure hadn't turned out how he'd expected it to, but at the moment, he didn't feel anything, just a cold emptiness that froze him to the spot as time ticked away.

He blinked and realized that it was best to go.

With a face stony with his anger, he smiled politely and walked away.

Tori stared at the door, wondering why it hadn't slammed shut. She'd expected him to rant and rave. Instead, he'd quietly walked away.

What had she done?

She had said some harsh things to Russell, but she'd felt she needed to say her piece. She loved Russell, and had known it for a while now, but she didn't want to place herself in a relationship that might or might not have a future.

She knew he loved her, but that love scared her. She would not end up like her mother, bowing to the wishes of a man who loved her, but controlled her.

If that meant that she had to lose what happiness she had, then she had to make the choice for herself.

She stared at the two pizzas in her hands and

the only thing she could think of was what she would do with the extra pizza with lots of cheese.

When she eventually moved, she headed slowly for the living room. She reached for the remote control and flicked through the channels, finding nothing of particular interest.

When the tears finally came, she was not surprised and she cried her heart out.

That night, Russell closed a chapter of his life. He'd toyed with calling Tori, but decided against it. He didn't think that much between them could be resolved. Tori's focus on her career seemed reasonable and to deny her the chance to touch the world with her gift would be like denying her life.

He loved music and could easily have made it his life, but unlike Tori, he didn't have the passion and fire for it. Onstage, those were the qualities she possessed that he knew would carry her far.

To be honest, he felt the same way about the work he did, especially now that his assignments focused on serious issues. He enjoyed the challenge of doing something investigative, something deep and probing. But he'd also come to appreciate the lighter stuff that allowed him to breathe fresh air. Too many of his assignments left him drained and feeling dirty on the inside and out. After those assignments, he often needed something to help restore his faith in a higher power.

He needed to get out of New York, needed to bury himself in a story that would require every hour of his time. He needed to forget. At first, he'd thought about taking a few weeks off and going to Barbados, but there, with nothing to do but swim and relax, he would spend too much time thinking about her.

That would not do.

His plan was simple. Engross himself in his work and purge Victoria Matthews from his soul.

He picked up the phone and dialed his boss's number. An hour later, he packed his bag and made arrangements for a colleague to take care of his apartment. He and his photographer would be leaving for London tomorrow evening and then on to Africa. He'd be there for a few months and he would bring back the best story he could about the small African nation still in unrest.

Already the adrenaline had started to flow and ideas on how to set out getting the story swirled chaotically in his mind. He headed for his laptop, needing to get all the ideas down and create some semblance of order. He'd browse the Internet to get as much background information as possible.

His excitement and focus were so intense that when the phone rang several hours later, he didn't hear it, his only thoughts on the tasks ahead.

Nothing else mattered.

* * *

Tori sat at her piano, the only thing that offered her comfort. After a night out with Rachel, she'd just wanted to be alone.

For a while, she'd enjoyed the night, the first time she'd been out in a month with someone besides Russell. But as the night progressed she'd soon lost interest and wanted to return home.

She had danced a lot, had been in great demand, but the arms holding her had not been the ones she wanted. Each man she'd danced with had eventually morphed into a man with dreadlocks and eyes that revealed every emotion.

At one point she'd actually contemplated going home with what's-his-name, the accountant. Handsome and really nice. Too nice…and boring.

But then she realized the reality of who she was. She could never give herself to anyone that lightly.

So she sat and played and wrote a song that she needed to put on paper. It was strange that times like these gave rise to masterpieces. All through history, artists often created their best work during their lowest times.

Maybe she could make a hit out of this one.

In the early hours of the morning when she could no longer stay awake, she headed to her bedroom and crawled into her empty bed.

The phone's luminous keys glowed in the night and the temptation to dial the number and apologize became too powerful to ignore. If they intended to move on with their lives, she owed him an apology. She'd been downright mean and Russell hadn't deserved it.

He loved her. There was no doubt in her mind that he did. But for her that was not all. If he'd given the slightest indication that he'd give his full support to her and her music, she would have willingly continued with the relationship.

To commit to him would have been to give too much of herself.

Tori saw how his face lit up whenever he talked about his nephews and niece. Russell wanted children and so did she. But not now, not at this moment when stardust glistened in her hands and the dream of standing before a large crowd and touching them with her music seemed in her grasp.

She wasn't sure why all these things were important to her, but these things were her, were all part of the woman she was and wanted to be.

Closing her eyes, Tori reached out instinctively, but realized no one was there.

She was alone.

Very alone.

In the distance, the moon hung in the sky, its rays caressing the gently undulating ocean. Tamara drew her husband to her, basking in the freshness of the soap he wore. They'd just made love for the second time that night, and her body felt exhausted but totally content. She'd been a bit worried about the intensity of their lovemaking when she'd discovered she was pregnant, but Dr. Haynes, whom Carla had recommended, had reassured them that a healthy sex life was not a problem, though she did tell them to be careful.

Tamara smiled, loving the feel of her husband's body. They'd been married just short of three years and still they had never grown tired of each other. She'd known him from their high school days.

A close friend of Shayne's, Kyle had disappeared from their lives after being involved in a serious accident. He'd come back into her life, blind and bitter, and she'd challenged him to be the man he could be.

Now Kyle was a different man. Always with a smile on his face, he embraced life with a passion that amazed people when they discovered he was blind.

Last year, he finally decided to go on tour. She'd taken two months off from her practice to go with him. She'd been confident that her assistant could handle the practice, and he had.

"What are you thinking about?" Her husband's voice broke the silence.

"You, me, life, how happy I am," she replied.

"Jared called today when you were in the office. He told me to give you his love."

"I can't believe I missed him. I'll give him a call in the morning. Anything wrong?" she asked.

"No, he is doing fine. He just called to let us know that he aced his presentation. One semester and he'll be back."

"I'm so proud of him," she said. She heard the pride in her husband's voice.

"I told him the good news. He told me we have to call his brother Jared Jr. Of course, he was kidding."

Tamara laughed. "So you didn't tell him we're using his middle name?"

"Not a word. He'll be surprised when he comes home for the summer. The baby's due just after he returns. And we did plan it to be our gift to him. You love him, don't you?" Kyle asked.

"You know I do. I consider him my son in every sense of the word."

"I'm glad. Just as you're going to love these babies."

"Yes, our babies. I'm scared, Kyle," she said.

"About the babies?" he asked.

"No, I'm not worried about them. We'll be careful this time. It's Russell," she told him, reaching for his hands to comfort her.

"I know there was something eating you," he said, his hand stroking her hair, giving her the comfort that she needed.

"I'm worried about him. He's met someone and for the first time, it's affecting him. I want him to find someone to love. Of course, I can't wait to meet this mystery woman. She seems to have lots of gumption. The last time I spoke to him, he was fine. Tells me he's over her, but all he talks about is her. I've never known Russell to be like that. He finds them, seduces them and then leaves them.

Now this woman has him tied up in knots and I don't know how to help him. I want him to find what we have. I want him to know love."

With that Tamara moved closer to her husband, straddling him with an ease that came with practice. His response came immediate and hard, and she reveled in the control she had over him.

When he slipped inside her she felt a joy she could not put into words.

So she responded the only way she could.

Her cry of ecstasy filled the room, only to be followed by her husband's own shout of intense pleasure.

Chapter 7

A year later

The sultry caress of Tori's voice still worked its magic. Russell had heard the song for the umpteenth time, but like each time before, it did not fail to move him. He knew she was singing about lost love. He knew she was singing about him and for him. Tori's first hit single continued to haunt him, even in the still hours of the morning when he tossed and turned and still reached for her.

A year had passed since he'd last seen her in person. He'd seen the official announcement on the television about her record deal, and he'd been privy to all the pre-release hype.

Her face graced the covers of magazines and newspapers, including his, and now her image stared down at him from a billboard along the motorway.

Russell had returned from Africa a few months before, exhausted, but proud about the work he'd done. His boss was already talking about awards, but winning an award for exposing exploitation and corruption would surely leave a bitter taste in his mouth.

Easing off the accelerator, he traveled the two blocks north before entering the newspaper's parking lot, and his reserved space.

Five minutes later, he was sitting at his desk, sipping a macchiato and enjoying the rich caramel taste, when the intercom buzzed.

"Yes, Russell."

"Russell, Brenda here. Can you come to my office when you get the chance?"

"I can come now."

"Good, I hoped you'd say that."

As he strolled down the corridor, he wondered what could be so urgent for the boss to call him this early. He usually heard from her later in the day, but rarely at this time of morning.

When he arrived at her office, Brenda's perky secretary immediately showed him in.

Brenda greeted him, her hand over the phone's mouthpiece. "'Morning. Give me a minute. I'll be done soon."

The call lasted exactly three minutes and twenty seconds, but when she gave him her full attention, she didn't waste time with pleasantries.

"Russell, I have a special assignment for you," she said.

He felt the familiar rush of excitement. Brenda's "special assignment" usually meant traveling.

"So where am I flying to this time?" he asked.

"I thought you'd be the perfect candidate for this job since it'll give you a chance to see your family. You can even take a week off when the festival is over."

"Festival?" he asked. He knew that it wasn't time for Crop Over.

"Yes, you're going to the Barbados Jazz Festival. We want you to cover the festival in general, but we also want you to do a feature on Tori Matthews. Her agent has offered us an exclusive interview with her."

At the look on his face, she asked, "You know who Tori Matthews is, don't you?"

"Yes, I know who she is. I don't want to do the assignment."

"You don't want to do it? I thought you'd jump at this opportunity to see your family. You haven't been home since your sister's wedding and that's almost four years ago."

"Brenda, I'd prefer not to go. Let someone else do the assignment. I'm sure Marco would jump at the opportunity to go."

"I'd be willing to give it to someone else if it weren't so important and the record company likes your style. Of the editors we suggested, they stated clearly they wanted you to do it. It's not my fault you're the best around here." She smiled, her voice teasing.

"So I have no choice," he replied.

"Let's not go there, Russell." The smile disappeared. "I just want you to be the professional I know you can be. I want you on the job, but if you really don't want to, then I'll see what I can do. I know you have some personal reasons for not going home, but maybe it's time you work whatever it is from your system. I know that something is bothering you. You're doing your work, but not out of enjoyment anymore. And I'm saying this not as your boss, but as your friend," she said. She reached over the desk and held his hands, squeezing them to offer some comfort.

"Okay, I'll think about it," he replied reluctantly.

And think about it he did. Thoughts of seeing Tori kept him awake long into the night and when he awoke the next morning, grumpy and hating his job, he knew exactly what he would do the moment Brenda had asked him.

He would go to the island.

The prospect of facing Tori didn't deter him. He wanted to see her and knew that when he left for the island he would be in full control. He had every intention of getting her back in his bed, by hook or…by crook—whatever worked.

He would call Tamara and Carla and tell them about his visit. He couldn't wait to see the family, and he knew he'd have to face his brother. Their talk was long overdue.

He'd made good for himself. He was working at one of the leading newspapers in the world… and he was happy.

Yeah, he didn't have the woman he wanted to spend the rest of his life with, but that would surely come with time. As sure as the sun rose each morning.

He slipped from his bed and dialed Brenda's number.

"Yes, Russell," she said. "I've already asked my secretary to book your flight for next Monday. You need to be there a few days before the jazz festival begins. Give you some time to meet the beautiful Tori Matthews."

They chatted a bit longer, but Russell made sure Brenda had no clue about the trepidation he felt at the visit.

He tried at all times to remain calm and neutral, but only time would tell.

The next few weeks were going to be interesting, very interesting.

Tori rested her head back on the seat and closed her eyes. Exhaustion seeped through her body and she knew she should sleep on the four-hour flight to Barbados. She felt uneasy about the trip. Of course, it wasn't her first performance since her album's release during the summer, but it would be her first in front of a large crowd. She'd done the late-night-television circuit and a few daytime shows, but her performances this time would be at the large indoor stadium named after a famous Barbadian cricketer knighted by Queen Elizabeth II.

Barbados.

Russell.

The two words were synonymous. From the time her management had told her she'd be performing at the island's annual jazz festival, she experienced discomfort. Fortunately, Russell still lived in the U.S., so there was no worry that she might pass him on the streets or in the hotel where she was staying. She'd spend the next week enjoying the island, performing at the two engagements, and then back to the U.S. to work on the video for her second single.

She thought of how much her life had changed during the past year and she couldn't believe it. The studio sessions, the interviews and all the other things that were part of her promotion had served to teach her most of what she needed to know about the music business.

She never lacked companionship during the day, but at nights she returned home alone. In those still hours of the morning when she lay awake, her memories of Russell remained vivid and clear. In those moments, Tori realized how much she missed him.

Sometimes, she wondered if she'd made the correct choice, but when she reflected on what she'd achieved, she realized that she'd made a choice she could live with.

She'd allowed logic to control her decision, but her emotions often betrayed her whenever his image flashed in her mind.

Next to her, her manager, Shanna, snored softly. The others were a few seats back. She stretched her legs out and lowered the seat. She could get accustomed to this. First class travel had its advantages. She remembered the tightness of sitting in economy. For her, those days were over and she felt a wash of sadness at what she had left.

The girl she had been no longer existed. One thing she did hope was that she remained humble and levelheaded. She didn't want to become a spoiled diva. The term *diva* alone brought images of angry, tantrum-inclined singers, but she could see how easy it could be to become that kind of person.

In the past few months she'd grown in confidence and on several occasions found herself forgetting that the people who worked around her were people with feelings and not individuals to do her bidding.

Tori had stopped herself in her tracks and brought herself back down the ladder. She always wanted to treat people around her with respect.

She was looking forward to making her new music video on the island. After the festival, a film crew would arrive for a three-day shoot. She'd heard so much about the island, and when she suggested the video be done there, those in charge had agreed. She'd been pleasantly surprised.

The president of the record company had intimidated her a bit at first, but then she realized that he'd signed her for her talent and she owed him nothing more than the best album she could make. She had no doubt that he'd made a lot of money off her.

Tori closed her eyes, willing herself to sleep. She was tired and the next few days were going to be difficult. She knew she'd enjoy being on the island, but she realized she'd have little time to rest.

Fortunately, Russell didn't do the social stuff. She didn't even know which newspaper wanted an exclusive. All she was told was that she had to accommodate a reporter and a photographer.

But have no fear, she'd put on her best smile and give them exactly what they wanted. It was all part of being the singer she always wanted to be. For little girls' dreams didn't always come true.

For her, they did.

Tori emptied her mind of all thoughts and before she realized it, she was fast asleep.

When she woke a few hours later, the plane was taxiing on the runway.

She'd arrived in Barbados.

* * *

Russell closed the door behind him and entered the house. No one welcomed him. He'd left the cameraman back at the hotel and immediately driven the hired car to the Knight plantation.

No one knew about his arrival. He wanted to surprise his brother and then he realized something important. This house was no longer theirs. Shayne was married and had a wife.

He heard the scamper of footsteps before he saw the person, and when his nephew Darius turned the corner, he almost broke into laughter at his nephew's expression.

The boy came to an abrupt stop and cocked his head to one side.

"I know you," he said, not a hint of a smile on his face.

"You do?"

"Yeah, you're my Uncle Russell."

"And you must be Darius?"

"I am Darius Shayne Russell Knight. I have Daddy's name and your name."

Russell couldn't explain the emotion he felt, but he started to get choked up. He never knew Shayne had honored him in that way.

Darius stepped forward. "It's good to meet you. Dad's in the study working. I'm sure if I go with you, he'd let us in. He told me to leave a few minutes ago since I was asking too many questions. He tells me the only way I can learn is by asking questions, and when I do, he tells me I'm asking too many. I never know what to do," Darius said with a sigh.

Russell couldn't help smiling.

"Well, come follow me." And he reached out his hand and took Russell's.

On the way down the familiar corridor, his nephew kept up the meaningless chatter about everything that was happening in his life at the moment.

When they reached Shayne's office, he knocked and then pushed the door.

"Darius, didn't I tell you I had a lot of work to do?" Shayne scolded.

Darius grinned. "Yes, Dad, but I couldn't be rude and leave Uncle Russell at the door."

Silence.

"Uncle Russell?" Shayne asked and then looked up to face them.

"Russell," he said. His voice had turned hesitant. He stood and walked out from behind the desk.

"Russell," he repeated, coming closer. He'd quickly regained his composure. "Why didn't you tell me you were coming? I'd have picked you up at the airport."

And then Russell felt his brother's arms around him and he knew he'd come home.

"It's taken you long enough to get here. But I'm glad you came. Darius and Carla have been asking about you. You'll be able to see your niece. She's a beauty. Looks just like Tamara when she was young. Don't know how that happened, but I'm sure when she gets older she'll either look like Carla or me. Or even you. It's all so unpredictable."

"Where is Carla?" Russell asked. He still couldn't believe he'd finally made it home. Shayne finally released him from the hug and he stepped back. His brother's warmth had been a bit too comfortable. He didn't want to be reminded about the past.

"She left to go to a meeting at Darius's school. She'll be back in a few hours. Lynn-Marie is with her so you'll get to see your niece later. You can tell me what you're doing in Barbados. I hope you can stay the night?"

"If it's not an imposition, I'd love to stay."

"Of course not, Russell. This is your home."

"I know, but you have a family now. This is your home."

"We're living in the west wing, so you can still use the room you had. How long are you staying?"

"I'm here for a week or two for the jazz festival. I have to do a feature for my newspaper," Russell replied.

"Good, you can stay here. I won't have my brother staying in a hotel. Where's the crew staying?" Shayne asked.

"It's just my cameraman. But I'm sure he'll be happy to know we won't be sharing rooms. He's been talking about all the girls he plans to meet… and bed."

Russell glanced over at his nephew, but though the boy was looking at them intently, Russell was sure Darius didn't have a clue what they were talking about.

"You have a fine son," Russell said. "And yes, it'll be nice to sleep in my old room."

"Good, then that's solved. You hungry? I know that you wouldn't have got much on the plane."

"I'm starving and could eat a horse," Russell replied.

Darius laughed. "Well, you have lots of choices, Uncle Russell. Just don't eat my horse."

"So you're like your dad. You love riding? Want to come riding with me one morning?"

"For real, Uncle Russell? We can go riding?"

"Yeah, once your dad says that it's fine."

"You were always almost as good a rider as I am, so your taking Darius is not a problem," Shayne responded.

"Almost as good as you are? I'd have said better."

"Better than the man who taught you? You must be kidding."

"Okay, I admit it. You're better, but right now, I'd prefer to get something to eat. I'm starved."

"Come, I'm sure I can still whip up something for you. It's Ms. Brown's day off."

"Ms. Brown?"

"Oh, you won't know her. Gladys has retired to a life of bliss. She's probably watching those infernal soap operas she loves." Shayne's tone softened as he spoke of Gladys.

"You can go up to her suite and see her when you're done. We sent her on a cruise with a friend when she retired and by the time she returned we'd decorated part of the east wing for her."

"Can I go with him, Dad?" Darius asked.

"Sure you can. Just make sure you're on your best behavior."

"I will, Dad."

"Now, come, let's go get something for your uncle to eat before he expires," said Shayne, rustling his son's hair.

An hour later, Russell sat on a chair in Gladys's room, listening to her talk about Tamara and the new baby. He couldn't wait to see his sister, but knew he'd have to wait for the next day. Tamara lived in the central parish of the island, and he really didn't feel like driving that far tonight. He'd call her tonight and visit her tomorrow.

He looked at Gladys, noticing for the first time how much she'd changed. In the three years since he'd last seen her, she'd definitely aged.

Immediately, he knew something was wrong.

"What's wrong, Gladys?" he asked.

"I could never hide anything from you. You know me better than the others."

"What's wrong, Gladys?" he insisted.

"Cancer…but I'm fine. I had a mastectomy and

it has taken care of the problem. For a while, I suppose. But with cancer you can never know what could happen."

"You're going to be fine, Gladys. I'm going to make sure of it," he said.

"I know God's going to take care of me, Russell. He's the healer. I hope you still go to church?"

He didn't know how to answer. Only knew that he'd hurt her with his response, but knew his silence would tell her the truth. "I've been busy. Sometimes I work on Sundays."

Her response didn't surprise him.

"You're finding excuses to tell me, Mr. Knight. I ain't bring you up that way. You know what God expects of you. You don't give me no excuses. I would take you cross my lap and give you a whooping."

Russell could tell she was angry. She always reverted to the local dialect when she was.

How many times had he heard those words before? Too many to imagine. And maybe he'd taken advantage of her during his early teen years. But he loved her.

"Make me one promise," Glady continued. "If anything happens to me, you won't be angry with God, but I want you back at church. Just go sometimes and it would make a world of difference."

"I promise," he said with hesitation. He'd do anything to make this woman happy.

"Good. That's all I want to hear. So, what brings you back to these shores?" she asked.

"I have to cover the jazz festival and have an interview with a new singer from the U.S.," he replied.

"Oh, your old girlfriend?" She giggled like a schoolgirl.

"Tamara's big mouth."

"She was worried about you, Russell, so she came to talk to me."

"I'm a big man. There's no need for her to worry about me," he argued.

"Yeah, you're a big man, but we love you so don't expect us to not worry."

"But things have changed."

"Yes, a lot has changed. Yeah, Shayne and Tamara are married now. But the only change I don't like is that you're not here," she insisted.

"But my work is in New York," he replied.

"I know your work's there. But it shouldn't stop you from coming home to the people who love you. I know you and your brother have things to work out, but you can't do it from over there. You not Bajan anymore?"

"Of course, Gladys. I know who I am and where I've come from. I may live in the U.S., but early in the morning I can still smell the freshness of the ocean breeze."

"Well, you need to work out whatever's happening between you and Shayne. I may not be around for too much longer, and I want my family here."

"New York's only a stone's throw away."

"But you have your life there. No need for you to worry about an old woman like me."

"That's why I didn't know you were ill. You didn't want to tell me," he said.

"And what would you have done? Come back home even though you don't want to? I would never intrude on your happiness."

"Intrude on my happiness? I'm sad, Gladys. Sad that you were ill and didn't give me the choice to be here. You made it for me."

There was silence in the room. He wished he could pull his words back.

"I'm sorry, Russell. I shouldn't have left you out of this," she said, and reached over and touched him.

"I didn't mean to snap at you. I love you, Gladys. You're the only mother we know. And I don't care where in the world I am. You don't do this to me again."

"I won't," she replied. Her breathing was labored.

"Good. Now that we've got that out of the way, I'm going to leave you and let you get some rest. I need a shower and some sleep. I promise I'll come see you in the morning."

"I am feeling a bit tired. I'll take my medication and get some sleep, too."

"I'll see you in the morning." He stood and bent to hug her. "I love you."

"I love you, too," she responded, her eyes already closed. She lay quietly and he stared at this gentle woman whom he cared about more than life itself.

Russell sat in the chair next to her bed and slowly gave in to the jet lag he was suffering.

He'd take a bath later. For now, he just wanted to be next to Gladys.

He needed to draw on her strength.

For at the moment, he wasn't feeling very strong.

Chapter 8

The sun rose with its usual excitement, its rays already eager to warm the slight chill of the early morning air.

Tori looked out to sea, watching the waves as they slowly made their way to the shore only to gently caress it before retreating the way they'd come.

Her thoughts lacked the peace of mind she'd grown accustomed to over the past few months. For a while, she had thought of Russell day and night, until she wondered if she'd ever get over him.

But she'd finally taken some measure of control. Her dreams of him had faded…but not completely. Sometimes, in the stillness of the lonely nights, she'd inhale his scent, and reach for him, only to realize he was not there.

When the phone rang, she turned away from the window, reaching for the cordless handset.

It was her manager, her voice, as always, controlled and professional. "You're still meeting us for breakfast in the restaurant by the pool?"

"Is that a question or statement?"

"Call it a reminder. Don't want you to miss our meeting with the reporter. I know you don't like it, but this is a pretty important exclusive that you're doing. Any artist would give her weight in gold to have this kind of promotion at the beginning of her career."

Tori sighed. "I know what you mean and I understand. I'm trying hard to forget the problems I've been having with reporters and the paparazzi. I knew I'd have to give up some of my privacy, but didn't expect it to be so bad."

"Look at it this way. The fact that they are all trying to interview you says something about the appeal you have. I promise you, we can deal with it. In a few months they'll be running after the latest wonder."

"Okay, I'm going in the shower now. Nine o'clock, right?" she asked.

"Yeah, I'll see you."

When the phone clicked, she placed it on its cradle.

* * *

The sweet Soca music of the island flowed from the speakers placed strategically around the restaurant. Russell checked his watch. Ten minutes before she walked through the door directly in front of him. She would be angry. He knew it; knew her enough to know she'd not take his deception lightly.

But he really wasn't being deceitful. He was just doing his job, and he didn't owe her any notification of who he was. He'd made it quite clear he didn't want his name mentioned. He planned on surprising her. Her reaction would give him a good gauge of her feelings for him.

The slight commotion at the entrance of the door drew his gaze.

It was Victoria Matthews.

He immediately noticed the changes.

Her hair had grown longer, much longer. When they were lovers, it had just reached the curve of her shoulder. Now it flowed down her back as she turned her head to chat with the man next to her.

The woman who walked toward him also moved with purpose and maybe a slight attitude. He hoped that her success had not transformed her into a diva.

From the periphery of his vision, he saw the slightest of movements. A small puppy raced into the restaurant, a little girl following after.

With an ease and grace that he'd always associated with her, she bent and reached for the pup, holding it, its tail wagging a hundred miles per hour.

"Thank you, miss," the little girl said. "I can't get Shaggy to stop running away."

"Maybe if you take her outside to run around she won't try to run away."

"My mommy tells me I need to keep her in our room since I just got her a few days ago, and she isn't trained. But I'll take care of her when we get home. We're leaving today."

"Good, then I must say goodbye to you and Shaggy. Was it your birthday?"

"Yes, I was ten and it was my mother's birthday so we are both celebrating."

"Good. I want to wish you a happy birthday."

"Thank you. You're as pretty as you are on television."

"I am?"

"Yes, my dad says you're the prettiest singer."

"Well, you must thank your dad for me. Enjoy your trip back home and take care of Shaggy. She's a lovely dog."

He watched as Tori placed the dog in the girl's hands and smiled before she glanced up. In that instant, their eyes met, not a gentle lingering glance, but a slam-in-the-chest kind of stare.

For the briefest of moments she seemed to stumble and lose her composure, but immediately a smile masked her face, a smile that didn't reach her eyes.

She turned to the woman next to her and asked a question. When she looked in his direction again, Russell saw a quick flash of fire and then the smile was back.

They stopped in front of his table. Russell stood. Gladys would be proud of him.

He chided himself. A random thought, but he knew that it was more than that. Being near Tori affected him more than he had expected.

No, he was lying to himself. He'd known that this would happen as surely as he knew his legs would be trembling. He waited for them to sit, hoping they'd not notice his slight discomfort.

He quickly joined them, feeling the jolt of awareness when her leg touched his.

Why did she have to sit right next to him?

"Miss Matthews, I'm glad you could come and meet with me. My newspaper feels honored that you agreed to the interview."

"Russell, come off it. There is no need for the formality. Shanna, Russell and I have been friends for some time. I am, however, surprised that I didn't know he was going to be the reporter following me around," Tori said. She'd regained her composure quickly.

"It's nice to see you, Tori. It's been a long time."

"True, I see you've been doing well."

"And you. Your face seems to be permanently fixed to my television," Russell said.

"As you know, all part of the promotion," she said.

"Good, now that you've met each other, I'll take my leave," Shanna said. "Tori, we can discuss the particulars at breakfast tomorrow and I'll go see if I can get rid of this headache."

"I'll call you as soon as I get up. When is rehearsal scheduled for?" Tori asked, glancing instinctively at her watch. "I don't want to be late."

"Ten o'clock. You still have a few days before the festival is officially opened."

"Okay, I'll call you as soon as I wake."

With that Shanna smiled and walked away briskly, the epitome of efficiency.

For what seemed like hours, there was silence. He wanted her to be the first to speak. He needed the time to observe her. Every movement expressed a nuance of emotion.

Now he could tell she was angry. With her manager gone, she didn't need to hide her true feelings.

"What are you doing here, Russell? I'm hoping this isn't some crazy joke," she spouted, her eyes darkened with emotion.

She was beautiful.

"You should know that I never play games or joke. For now, I'm on assignment, so we'll get down to why you're here. I was informed by my chief that since I'm a Barbadian I'd be the best person for the job. I can't let personal issues affect how I do my job and I'm hoping the same goes for you."

She inhaled deeply and he could see her conscious effort to regain control.

"Okay, I'm just frustrated. I'm looking forward to the festival and being one of the headliners. I'm sorry I accused you of playing games. Tell me what you want from me and I'll see how I can accommodate you."

"Good, I'm hoping that we can do an article and photo spread that will make you proud," he said.

"Thanks. I have no doubt that whatever you do will be excellent," she commented.

For the next hour, Russell informed Tori about the plans for the few days, when he would be with her. The conversation was easy, but between them the tension sizzled.

Russell could not help but be amazed by how much Tori had learned in the past month. She already had a sound grasp of the industry and the part she had to play. Her knowledge and rapport belied her inexperience and he remembered she'd been a singer way before this contract.

When he took the final sip of his cup of tea, he noticed that she shivered. *Good sign.*

"It's been nice chatting with you," Tori finally said. "I'm sure the article is going to be a good one. However, I have to get to my room. I traveled all day yesterday and because the flight was delayed I'm beat. Jet lag is now beginning to kick in. I'll be ready tomorrow for the rehearsal. Just call me when it's time to leave." Tori stood, ready to hightail it to her room. So he still had an effect on her.

Before she could go, he stood and reached for her hands, lifting one to his lips.

She pulled her hands away.

"Tori, I'm going to promise you one thing. You asked earlier if I was playing games with you. I'm going to answer the question because it's only polite. I'm definitely not playing games. I recognized something tonight. You want me."

At her raised eyebrow, he continued. "And I know I want you. So whatever is to happen will happen. And I promise you this much—we'll be lovers again before you leave the island."

Tori tried to speak, but only managed to splutter.

"No need to respond, my dear. But you have a good night's sleep."

With that he turned and walked away, knowing that she'd be looking at him.

Games indeed. Miss Tori Matthews was in for a big surprise. He had every intention of keeping his promise.

When Tori closed the door behind her she was fuming. What was Russell up to? He'd changed. The man she'd fallen in love with had been gentler, sensitive. This man was different. He seemed harder, determined.

She didn't stand a chance.

But she had every intention of fighting him. She would not succumb to his seduction.

If that's what he had planned.

She wasn't the same love-struck individual she had been a year ago. She'd grown. She was now a successful singer with a promising future and she had every intention of being in control of her life and no man was going to stop her.

Her body shivered.

Already she was losing it.

Why did he have to come back into her life at this time?

She shivered again.

Images of them together flashed in her mind.

For too long she'd felt empty, incomplete. He'd done that to her. No, she'd done that to herself. She was the one who'd walked away.

She had success now, and she loved being a part of the vibrant world of music.

But often while she sat in meetings or at home learning the lyrics for her latest song, she'd ache all over, the memory of Russell's gentle touch vivid in her memory.

Tonight the feeling was the same. The ache for him started in the usual way. The shivering body and then the warmth slowly spreading through her, circulating in her veins until it reached the core of her womanhood and she shivered with silent release.

Maybe she should simply just give in to the inevitable. The island was perfect for romance.

She'd give him what he wanted and in time she'd satiate her ache for him.

Maybe this time she'd be able to purge him from her system completely.

Maybe this time she'd be able to be more of the woman she wanted to be.

But for some reason she knew that without him, she'd been incomplete. There was no hope for them when Russell didn't want the life she craved, the life that was now hers.

She picked up the phone, and dropped it again. Maybe a talk with her mother would help her to see things a bit more rationally.

The phone rang for a while before it cut into her mother's voice.

She returned the handset to the base, sighing.

What was she going to do?

She knew what would relieve the stress she was feeling.

A shower.

But when she entered the shower, an image of her and Russell making love with the water cascading around them forced her to stop.

He'd worked himself into her system and she knew there would be no sleep tonight.

As she dried her skin minutes later, she willed herself to focus on the rehearsal the next day.

She ran through several of the songs before she slipped into a large T-shirt and drifted into a restless sleep.

Her last thought was that tomorrow would be another day to resist his intensity.

And she didn't know how successful she was going to be.

During the night, Russell did not sleep. Not because of his dreams about Tori, but because of the discomfort that came from his constant state of arousal. His desire for her intensified and reluctantly he'd taken matters into his own hands.

But nothing came close to satisfying his craving for Tori. He'd forced himself not to go to her room. He knew that if he knocked on her door, he'd be waking up next to her this morning.

But no, she would be the one to come to him. His willpower was stronger and he knew it; she knew it. It was only his determination and her pride that had left her sleeping alone last night.

He smiled. This was going to be fun. The hunt was on.

He'd claimed the role of hunter, but Tori would learn her role as the prey in time.

He had no doubt that she'd eventually come to him, and the thought made him stiff and hard again.

He'd planned to return to the Knight plantation, but for tonight sleeping at the hotel had been a better idea.

Later today, they would be going to the small theater where the rehearsal would take place.

On Saturday, a week away, she'd be performing

along with a few regional artists at the Sir Garfield Sobers Gymnasium. On Sunday, they were going to "Jazz on the Hill," an outdoor event held at one of the island's national parks in the north.

Ironically, before he'd left for the U.S., he'd never attended any of these events. He'd been so focused on his studies he'd had no time for pleasure.

Now as Russell looked back on his teenage years, he realized how strange he'd been. Yes, at school he'd been like any normal boy. He'd played sports, but his goal had been his academic success and it had taken so much from him not to go to med school when he'd completed high school. It had always been in his plans…and Shayne's. To say that his brother had been disappointed at his choice would be simplifying the situation.

Though his brother had told him how he felt and that the choice was his, Russell could not fail to see the disapproval.

Now, on reflection, he realized he'd done it to force some sort of human emotion from his brother. Back then Shayne had focused on two things. Raising his siblings and the plantation.

Russell loved his job, so in some ways he'd discovered something he really liked, and being a doctor had been what Shayne wanted for him.

He did, however, thank his brother for not insisting that he go to med school. If Shayne had insisted he probably would have gone, even if it had been after he objected.

There was no one in the world he loved more than his brother and sister.

He glanced at his watch. It would soon be sunrise, and time to get up. He wanted to visit Tamara this morning. Shayne had given him directions and he'd called her. He needed to talk to her... about Tori.

Sitting on the balcony of his room, he watched the sun come up, took a few hours more of sleep and by nine o'clock he was pulling out of the hotel's exit on his way to St. Thomas.

A half hour later, he turned into the driveway of his sister and her husband's home.

Immediately, the front door opened and a beaming Tamara raced outside. Behind her, Kyle and a large dog stood.

When Tamara reached him and gripped him in a tight hug, he felt the comfort of her embrace.

"Russell Knight, I'm very annoyed. Coming to Barbados without calling and letting me know. What kind of brother are you?" she scolded.

"I wanted to surprise you."

She smiled, stepping back to look at him. "Fine, I'm surprised. I'm so glad to see you. Kyle is as excited as I am to have you visit, aren't you, Kyle?"

"Russell, like my wife said, it's a pleasure to finally have you in our home. I know we would have met at the wedding, but you really didn't stay in Barbados too long. I hope you're here for a longer time."

"I'm here for just over a week, but I'm open to staying a bit longer. I'm here on business."

"Okay, come, let's not stay out here and chat," Tamara said. Russell could tell she could not contain her excitement. "We can do that inside. I know you haven't eaten breakfast, so I made sure I did your favorite. Or what used to be your favorite."

"Fish cakes and bakes, corn pops and some of your best lemonade."

"Does that mean things haven't changed? I was here thinking that my brother had become all Americanized."

"Definitely not. I may live in the U.S., but I'm still very much a Bajan at heart. I love living in New York, but I still think of Barbados as home."

"Good to hear," she said.

When they reached the kitchen, the delicious scent made his mouth water, and his stomach grumbled. He hadn't realized how hungry he was.

"Tamara, I hope this is not an indication of how much you think I eat?"

"No, it's for all of us. Of course, Kyle has a healthy appetite. And you, despite your implications, know how to take care of your stomach. So come, let's sit, and then we can chat all we want. You have to tell me what you're doing here."

Russell poured himself a glass of lemonade, and filled his plate with bakes and fish cakes. While he ate, Tamara kept the conversation going. He could not help but observe his brother-in-law's ability during the meal. He remembered Kyle being one of the best young cricketers on the island. He'd heard about the accident that had almost killed him, but it was not until four years ago when his sister had called and told him about living next to Kyle that he'd realized Kyle's accident had resulted in his loss of sight.

After they were done, Kyle excused himself.

"Russell, I must get back to work. You know us writers. I have a deadline coming up in a few days. If you're still here after that, then I'm sure we'll get together. In fact next Sunday when I'll be all done, the guys are planning to hang out, so of course you're invited."

"I'll still be here," he replied.

"Good, I'm sure you and your sister have lots to talk about before your meeting, so I'll leave you to catch up. Please don't be a stranger. Our home is your home."

With that he turned to his wife. "I'll see you later, honey." He reached over and kissed her. "'Bye," he said, and was gone.

His sister's devoted gaze followed her husband until he exited the room and then she turned to Russell and said, "So, you plan to tell me what's going on? I'm quite aware who's one of the headline artists for the jazz festival."

"I was asked to do an exclusive on Tori for the newspaper. Since I'm Barbadian, my boss thought I was the ideal person to do the interview. It's not only about her, but the island must play an important part in the feature."

"So you're happy with what you're doing?" she asked.

"I'm definitely happy. Beats being a doctor any day."

She laughed. "You know Shayne only wanted the best for you."

"Yes, I know. I know I was too hard on him. I plan to have a serious chat with him while I'm here."

"Good, you need to make peace with him. He misses you. I miss you," she said.

"So, how're the babies?" he asked.

"Babies? Danielle and Devon aren't babies anymore. They're almost seven months and I'm convinced Devon is ready to walk. They're both asleep. Kept us awake all night and now sleeping."

"So you're happy?"

"Yes, I'm happy. Kyle is a wonderful man. I didn't think that marriage could be so good. I was down a bit when I miscarried during my first pregnancy, but God has blessed me with a boy and a girl. What more could I want?"

"Kyle seems cool, safe. I'm looking forward to getting to know him. The man to capture my sister's heart must be special."

"So, who has captured my brother's heart?" she asked.

"Need I tell you?"

"So that's why you're here."

"No, it's an assignment for the newspaper, but since I'm here, I intend to use my powers of persuasion to convince her that she can't live without me."

"So my brother's in love."

"Seems that way," he said and then paused. "Yes, I think I'm in love. Still not sure what love is, but if it feels like your gut is ripping out, then I definitely am. But I understand where she's coming from. She has her dream and I tried to make her give it up. I'm having mine. I *was* being selfish. Of course, I have my work cut out for me now. She's definitely wary."

"I'm sure you'll find a way to convince her you love her."

"She knows I do," he said.

"Yes, but you have to convince her."

"But she's the one who decided to go ahead with this singing thing. I wanted to marry her," Russell argued.

"See what I mean? You may feel that you've wronged her, but you still look at what she's doing as her 'singing thing.' You don't respect what she's doing. How'd you like to give up your job and let her do her singing? And I can tell from your expression that you'd go crazy."

"Okay, okay, you made your point. I'm aware that I'm being selfish. Seems that I have a lot of thinking to do. Shayne. Now Tori. Maybe some good will come from all of this."

"Russell, you were never about maybe. If you want Tori in your life, I suggest you go after her."

"Well, sis, I have every intention of going after her."

"And remember, it's not all about sex."

"It isn't?" he teased, laughing. "I'm just kidding. It's not all about. About fifty percent?"

"You're crazy, you know."

"Yeah, just as crazy as you."

"It's really great to see you, little brother."

"By six minutes, only six minutes." He glanced at his watch, realizing it was time to go. "I'm going to have to go. Tori has a rehearsal this morning and I have to be there."

"You'll come back and see me."

"Of course, Tamara. I'm planning to stay on for a week or two after the festival is over. And I promised Kyle I'd come by. Have to make sure I bond with my sister's other half."

"You'll enjoy him. He's a bit serious at times, but that's what makes him who he is. And he's finally accepted his blindness and not trying to be a superstar."

"What about your other son? Jared?"

"He's doing fine. In a few months he'll be Dr. Austin. He plans to open his practice a year or so after he returns."

"It must feel strange having a son who's just a few years younger."

"It's cool. We're more like best friends. Kyle is

the real parent. He loves Jared as his own. I told him I don't want him to love Jared any less than how he loves those babies upstairs, but I don't think there is any need. They have a special bond that I know will always be there."

He glanced at his watch again. "Tamara, I really need to go. We'll definitely talk about this more." He stood, waiting for her to follow him.

"Of course, you'll have to keep me informed of your progress."

"Progress?" he asked.

What on earth was she talking about?

"Dummy, I mean with Tori," she said.

"I'll make sure I let you know since you'll only keep on asking."

"Good, come give me a hug before you go."

Tamara hugged him. "You take care of yourself," she said.

"I will, I'm coming back to see those cute babies of yours."

Minutes later Russell watched as she waved at him in the rearview mirror.

He could tell that Tamara was happy and totally in love with her husband. He was glad for her. She deserved only the best.

Why couldn't he have it like that? He wanted the same happiness for himself.

Ironically, when he thought of his university days, he remembered that wanting what Tamara and Kyle had had been far from his mind. Now, he'd become enchanted by the music of a sultry singer and the sway of hips that begged to be touched.

His body tensed as it did when he thought of her. He knew that the grin on his face went from ear to ear. He couldn't wait to see her.

Chapter 9

Onstage, Tori wished that the rehearsal would come to an end. It wasn't that she didn't mind, it was that Russell's probing eyes made her remember when they'd met and the first time they'd made love. The windows in his bedroom had steamed with the passion that had erupted between them.

Her final song for the rehearsal was a bluesy, haunting song of lost love and broken hearts.

Tori stopped, floundering on the words of a song she'd written and performed on several occasions.

"Tori, take a break. We'll start back in fifteen minutes," Carl, the stage director, said.

"Thanks, Carl. I'm a bit distracted. I'll be fine. A break must be what I need."

With that she left the stage and headed toward the washroom.

Inside, she washed her face and returned to the rehearsal room.

When she got there, several of the guys were not back and she glanced at her watch and realized that only five minutes had passed.

The only person sitting in the auditorium was Russell.

He looked around when she entered. He smiled, that warm smile that always reached his eyes. However, she saw more there, caution, distance. She felt the need to chat with him.

She moved in his direction, her heart racing. Maybe talking to him would help her to focus.

"So you made it?"

"Yes, I slipped in just after you started," he replied. "You're getting better. Stronger, more confident."

"I've been trying to improve," she said, the sarcasm evident.

"No need to be bitchy," Russell responded. "I'm just trying to be polite."

"I'm sorry. Put it down to being frustrated."

"So I'm frustrating you?" he asked.

"I didn't say that. Why would you think that?"

"You are frustrated. You're not focused. I don't have anything to do with that, do I?" he asked. He couldn't keep the smile off his face.

"Why should you?"

"Seems that you're going to respond to each of my questions with another question," Russell said.

"And why would I do that?" She paused and then she laughed. "Okay, I see what you mean."

"Well, we're going to have to continue this discussion after rehearsal. Come, go to lunch with me. We can talk about the interview I want to have and what questions you'll approve."

She didn't want to be with him. She wanted to be with him. Her mind was so damned confused. He was still doing it to her and she'd told herself she'd never let another man try to control her life.

Not that Russell wanted to control her life, but she felt as if she was losing a part of herself, her dream.

"Okay, we can do lunch." With that, she thought the best thing to do was retreat as quickly as possible. Thankfully, the men had returned and she nodded to Russell and walked quickly to the stage.

During this session, knowing who the source of her distraction was, she focused and gave herself totally over to the music.

Of course, she could feel his gaze on her, but she came back with her cloak of professionalism fitting neatly and refused to be distracted.

As she sang she remembered the first night they had met, the crowded club, the faint hint of tobacco lingering in the air.

She'd come a long way and she was proud of herself.

But she was worried; worried about the impact

of Russell's intrusion into her life and the way that even now, after a year, he rocked her world.

Two hours later, they sat in the tiny alcove of one of the hotel's restaurants.

"So what are you eating?" he asked.

"I'm not sure. What do you recommend?"

"The grilled salmon with vegetables looks good," he said.

"I was thinking about that, too. I'm still trying to eat healthier food. I've removed red meat from my diet."

"Good, I was hoping that my influence would be strong enough to make you eat well," he said.

"You'd be surprised what happens to a person when she becomes a singer. I have a nutritionist who makes sure I eat and exercise well. Have to keep up the Hollywood image."

He went silent for a moment. "Do you like it?" he finally asked.

"That's a difficult question to answer. I love some aspects. My life has changed significantly, but I feel stronger, more in control of my life. But I don't like the publicity, the paparazzi. I miss being able to go to the supermarket without worrying about my picture being taken. And don't talk about shopping. It's still not too bad yet, but I can see it getting worse."

"You don't seem too happy about all that's happening."

"Oh, don't get me wrong. I'm still enjoying the other aspects of this new career. I love the music I'm making and the fact that so many more people love my work. And the money isn't bad. I can do and buy lots of things I couldn't before. You should see the sports car I bought," she said.

"Now, I'll definitely take up the invitation. Promise me a drive and I'll be there as soon as we touch down in New York."

"I remember when you said you were going to buy a sports car as soon as you made it big," she observed.

"Oh, I'm not too far away from getting mine. Seems that we've both accomplished our goals."

"Yeah, seems that way," she said.

For a while there was silence. "I think about you a lot, Tori."

"I know. I think about you, too," she said.

Her response surprised him. Russell had not expected her to admit to anything. "We're a pack of messed-up individuals when it comes to our love lives."

"Couldn't disagree. Are you still angry with me about the choice I made?" she asked.

He could tell she needed reassurance; that her choice still caused her some internal conflict. "No, I'm not. I realize I was being selfish. I wanted my dream, but didn't want you to have yours. And yes, I was annoyed because it didn't take you long to decide to refuse my proposal."

"I didn't mean to hurt you. You know how I felt about you, but you knew I wanted to be a singer more than anything. At that time, I couldn't believe you wanted me to give it up."

"I realized I was wrong to expect that of you. You…" He stopped when the waitress came to take their order.

When she left, he continued. "Tonight, there will be no more talk about the past. Only the future and what it has in store for us."

"I agree. The future holds so much for both of us. Your career seems to be heading in the direction you wanted. I've seen several of your articles and they were all well written and hard-hitting. I particularly like the piece you did on the African nation. It must be a step down for you to have to do an assignment like this."

"Oh, definitely not. All articles help me to grow as a writer. I don't want to be stereotyped or pigeonholed."

"You plan on remaining at the newspaper or move into television?" she asked.

"I want to stay in the print media, maybe even write a book sometime. Since my brother-in-law is a famous writer, I'm sure he'll point me in the right direction."

"Who is he?" she asked.

"My brother-in-law? He's K.D. Austin."

"Come off it. Tamara is married to him? I didn't know he was Barbadian. I've read some stuff by him and discovered last year that he lives here with his wife, but I didn't make the connection. You didn't even tell me. But you've never talked about your family much," she said.

"I don't think that we had much time for much else, did we? But I promise to tell you all you need to know."

"That's what you always said when I asked about your family," she complained.

"Which suggests that in some ways I haven't changed completely. I promise to be the perfect gentleman in the future."

The waitress interrupted again, placing the delicious-smelling food before them. They both dug in with relish, only stopping occasionally to say something.

As they ate, the air between them sizzled. It was as if there was no need for conversation between them. Occasionally, their eyes met, his caressing her boldly, hers responding with a coquettish furtive glance.

Russell had no doubt where this night would end and the thought of making love to her made him uncomfortable.

Not that her eating didn't contribute to his discomfort. How many more times could he watch her lick her lips without taking her into his room and cooling the fire raging inside him?

Russell watched as her tongue flicked out to brush the frosting from the cake she was eating.

"Heavenly, there is nothing like a piece of chocolate cake," she said, taking another bite of the cake.

"I'm sure your manager won't be too happy with your eating like this."

"I'll be fine. I work out for one hour each day, so he knows I'm pretty disciplined. And I don't gain weight easily."

"I've noticed. You look as fine as you did a year ago. Some things haven't changed."

Russell signaled to the hostess who was passing by and requested the bill.

"Forgive me, I should have asked if there was anything else you wanted."

She didn't answer at first, but then she replied, "Yes, I want something else, but it sure can't be had here." Her voice was husky with desire.

"And what is that, may I ask?" His heart felt as if it would pop from his chest.

She leaned toward him. Her eyes were flushed, bold. "I want you to make love to me."

He looked at her intently, seeing the sincerity of her words in her smoldering eyes. It was a simple request, but one that held many repercussions. For a moment, he hesitated, but he wanted her too much to refuse.

"Then your wish is my command. The hostess should soon be back."

No sooner had he said the word than the woman appeared. Russell quickly signed the credit card slip, and placed that and a generous tip in the holder.

They reached his room in record time, stripping each other's clothes as soon as they entered through the door.

When Tori stood naked before him, he could not take his eyes off her. She was beautiful. He noticed some changes. Her gym time had definitely added some improvement, but he didn't want to spend time discovering those changes. All that could be done later.

Taking her hand, he led her to the bed. He wrapped his arms around her, lowering himself and taking her with him. They laughed. It was a game they'd played before.

Tori lay on top of him, and he drew her closer, almost as if they were one. For a while they lay there, getting accustomed to the feel of each other, savoring the quiet moments before they allowed the passion to explode.

Tentatively, he moved his mouth toward hers. She responded immediately so that when their lips touched, she allowed him access to her sweetness.

He drank from her, loving the soft groans that told him of her pleasure. He shifted her over, lying on top of her.

Raising himself on his arms, he moved downward, raining her neck with gentle kisses until he reached her breasts, ready and aroused with desire.

He placed one hard, dusky orb in his mouth and suckled on it, before he moved to the other.

And then he moved to her firm stomach, and then lower and lower.

His tongue worked its magic, knowing what pleased her. Her body contracted and released, her pleasure evident in her cries of ecstasy.

His tongue flickered and probed, tasting the tanginess of her vagina.

When her body began to shudder, he knew she was near release and he raised himself, capturing her lips in a deep kiss, and the same time plunging himself inside her.

The scream from her lips was one of total ecstasy. Immediately, her legs wrapped around him, drawing him nearer, and Russell almost lost it, but brought himself under control. He wanted this ride to last longer, but knew that with the simple touch of her hand he was a goner.

He established a steady rhythm, a simple but easy in-and-out, back and forth, but angling himself so that he touched the points of her highest sensitivity.

Tori was by no means a passive lover, so she joined him, urging him on until the ride became as wild as a rodeo.

With each stroke, Russell reveled in her tightness, her muscles gripping him tightly, allowing him to feel the soft friction of each movement.

And soon the end was near. His legs tightened and he could feel the pulsating of his penis.

When the end came, it came like an earthquake, shaking his body until he could no longer resist.

And Tori joined him, her own body shaking with the intensity of her release.

For a while, they held on to each other, allowing their bodies to calm and relax.

Russell shifted from on top of her, aware of his weight, but keeping her locked in his embrace. He loved these moments. Loved when the hot passion was all over, and all that was left was the gentleness of intimacy.

She nuzzled closer to him, her head against his chest. "I'm exhausted," was all she said, before she closed her eyes and promptly fell asleep.

For a while Russell lay there, his hand tenderly stroking her hair. He loved this woman more than life itself. For a man who hadn't known or cared much about love, he'd surely been taught a lot in a short space of time.

Love was no longer just a physical thing, but something deeper; something that touched a person's heart. He had finally been touched.

His last thought before he too drifted off to sleep was to wonder if she loved him as much.

The first thing Russell felt when he woke was the feel of soft cushions around him. He snuggled deeper under the covers, inhaling the familiar scent of…

His eyes flew open, immediately seeing the woman who lay next to him.

He smiled, moving closer to her. He placed his

hands around her. This was one of the things he missed most—waking up next to her. Tori had this way of curling herself around him like a comma, a tight comma, but he loved the feel of her against him.

For a while he stared at her, watching the gentle rise and fall of her breasts. Even now after having made love to her during the night he still wanted her.

He experienced the now familiar surge of arousal. He wanted her, wanted her with the aching that was not easy to describe or understand.

He'd had women before, but none that shook his world like Tori did. He'd messed up with his alpha-male attitude, but he knew he had a second chance and he didn't want to make the same mistakes. He knew when she woke, she'd not be too happy with what had happened between them.

Yes, she wanted him as much as he wanted her, but she didn't want to want him. Wanting him, loving him, to her, was like giving up her independence, and she wouldn't give that up easily.

Tori frustrated him, but he'd never been one to wait for what he wanted. If he saw something and wanted it, he went after it with a passion and intensity that ended in one result.

Tori stirred and her eyes flicked open. He saw the awareness and then a shadow came and his heart physically hurt.

"Tori, don't make this bad by regretting it."

"I don't regret it, but it shouldn't have happened."

"Isn't that the same thing?" he asked as his hand reached to touch her.

"No, I wanted to make love to you. You know it. I know it. But it's not going to change anything. I have my career and I have no intention of giving it up."

"We can compromise. We love each other."

"Do we? What I see between us are two healthy individuals who love to jump into bed with each other at the drop of a hat. Does that mean we love each other? I don't think so. We've been so into the passion that we haven't grown to know each other. And it's way too late for that," she argued.

"It is?" Russell asked. "You're not willing to give us a chance. Give us a chance to know each other. You're just going to give up?"

He reached for her, drawing her closer. "When I met you, I didn't know what would happen to us. I wasn't ready for any of this. I saw a beautiful woman and wanted her. Just as you wanted me."

At her frown, he continued. "But what I feel is more than that. I won't try to force you into anything that you don't want. I know that your music is the most important thing to you right now and—"

"See?" she interrupted. "You go jumping to conclusions. My music is important to me and I want to be the best damn singer I can be. But I want other things, too. I want children and a home filled with love. It's just that you want these on your terms and my choice doesn't matter."

She pulled away from him. "I need to get back to my room. There's a press conference this morning and then I have a rehearsal this evening."

"Of course, I'll be there. We still have to set up a proper time for your interview."

"No problem, I'll let you know."

Russell watched as she slipped from the bed and quickly dressed. When she reached the door, she turned.

"We'll work this out. I promise."

So there was hope for the two of them. Good. He had every intention of fighting for her. Despite her eloquent speech about their not loving each other, he knew better. It was not the hot sex between the two of them, but the way she made him feel when she was near.

Maybe they'd been a bit too physical, but he knew there was more. And Tori knew it, too. She was just trying to find justification to move on, but she knew there was no moving on.

With Tori gone, he jumped from the bed. He had lots to do today. There was the press conference and then he wanted to spend the rest of the day at the plantation. He wanted to take a ride on one of the horses. He hadn't ridden for a while and ached to feel the wind blowing through his hair. Maybe he could convince Shayne to come with him. His brother was an accomplished rider, and had made the Barbados team for show jumping, but had been unable to compete because of his commitment to his siblings.

Over the years Russell realized how much Shayne had given up to take care of them.

He knew there was part of him that had been unreasonable in his treatment of Shayne, but he'd still allowed himself to grow. At least that good had come out of his estrangement from his brother.

But he loved Shayne. Loved his brother more than he would ever love another man. Shayne was all he'd ever wanted to be, hands down.

Shayne had even given up going to college to take care of them, and for this he would be forever grateful.

At least Shayne had been lucky enough to find the perfect wife. And Carla *was* the perfect wife. His brother had changed. He seemed happier, more animated. The brother he remembered had been so serious about life.

In the shower, Russell enjoyed the feel of the water cascading from the faucet. He needed this. Needed to purge the consuming heat from his body.

Already he was thinking of making love to Tori again, but knew it wouldn't happen for a while. He knew Tori, knew that her pride wouldn't allow her to come to him, no matter how much she wanted him. And after tonight, she'd put up a wall that he'd have to jump over if he wanted to get in.

Well, she was in for a big surprise; he'd been a high jumper at school and nothing would stop him or his resolve to have her.

Tori Matthews was in for a big awakening!

Chapter 10

At the press conference at the Sandy Lane Hotel, Tori charmed the members of the press with her wit and professionalism.

By the time she stood and waved goodbye to the media and other VIPs who were there, everyone was eating out of her hand.

To Russell, that had always been her best asset. Of course, she could sing; her husky tone and range made her a singing diva. But infusing her vocal acrobatics with effervescent charm, she had the makings of a superstar.

The music she loved to write and sing was not for every audience, but she was realistic enough to know that R & B and pop music sold. Though she loved jazz, she embraced other kinds of music.

He couldn't wait to see her perform at the concert. He knew she'd be good, but he'd not seen her since that night more than a year ago when he'd been enchanted by her sultry torch song.

With the press dispersing, he moved toward her. He hoped she'd be willing to go with him. He wanted her to meet his family. When Tamara had called just after his shower, he'd not been surprised at her request to bring Tori over to the house. There was going to be a special family luncheon and they wanted him to be there. Of course, Tamara did not allow him to decline.

When Russell reached Tori, she glanced up, their eyes met and sparks flew.

"Russell," she said.

"Hi, you did well."

"Thank you," she replied.

"I came to invite you to lunch. My sister, Tamara, insisted that you come. I can't disappoint her."

"I don't think that's a good idea."

"She told me I can't come without you. You don't want to be held responsible for my demise, do you?"

"No, I don't." She paused for a moment. He could see she was torn by what to do. "I'll let my manager know. I'll have to be back by five o'clock for the rehearsal. It's the last one before the concert on Sunday night."

"I promise I'll have you there by four thirty. Don't want you to get in trouble."

She turned and he watched as she walked away. She spoke to the manager, smiled and then came back to him.

"Let's go. He's fine with it."

"Good, my sister and brother are looking forward to meeting you."

She did not respond. He wondered why but decided not to say anything.

They walked to the car Shayne had lent him. The drive to the Knight plantation was a quiet one. Tori's occasional questions about buildings or the occasional church broke the silence, but there was nothing to indicate that anything had happened between them the night before. If that was how she wanted it, then he had no problem complying. However, he knew this was all part of the game she didn't even realize she was playing.

When the car pulled into the almost three-hundred-foot driveway, he experienced that sense of pride he felt whenever he saw the plantation house.

It was awesome. And it was his home, his heritage. A few years ago, he had told Shayne he was signing over his right to the house to him, but his brother had refused, only eventually accepting his interest as a gift for Darius's and Lynn-Marie's trust fund.

The stately colonial design of the house almost transported them back in time, to an era that was not like this. Large jalousie windows that his brother had paid handsomely to restore gave the house a stately aura.

When the car pulled up, the first one out the door was Darius.

"Daddy, Daddy, Uncle Russell is here. And he has a pretty girlfriend with him."

Beside him, Tori stiffened, and he reached out to touch her, willing her to relax. When she exited the car, a genuine smile was plastered on her face and he knew she'd already been enchanted by Darius.

His nephew was handsome and Russell knew in the next few years he'd be breaking hearts.

He breathed in deeply. Maybe this lunch would turn out to be all right.

Tori couldn't help it. She'd fallen in love for the second time in two years with a Knight. This new charmer was the nephew of the man she loved. Ironically, she could see the similarities in the two.

"So what do I call her, Uncle Russell? Auntie Tori? When are you going to marry her? I love weddings."

Tori wasn't sure she wanted to respond to all the questions, but she didn't have a reply. "Tori will be fine."

"I'm not supposed to call adults by their first name. So I'll call you Auntie Tori since you're Uncle Russell's girlfriend."

She was about to say she wasn't Russell's girlfriend, but she stopped. Technically, she wasn't, but for a while they had been a couple. And "Auntie Tori" did sound important.

"Okay, Auntie Tori is fine."

"Cool," Darius replied. "Do you want to come and see my horse? She had a foal."

"I'd love to."

"Tori, are you sure you want to go," Russell asked.

"Of course, can't disappoint my new boyfriend."

"Uncle Russell, I like your girlfriend," Darius said, taking her hand and leading her away from the adults.

"Bring her back safe, Darius," said Carla.

"I will, Mom," he said, his face taking on a look of importance that made Tori smile.

On the way to the stable, Darius chatted about everything under the sun. She even got one of those knock knock jokes, but she was so enchanted by the little boy, she took part in the conversation willingly.

She wondered if she and Russell were to have a child whose features it would have. Would he resemble her or would the child carry the Knight look? Darius was definitely a Knight. He had that distinctive look of determination on his face that she saw in Russell and in Shayne. Even Tamara carried the look. And they all had that stubborn chin.

In the stable, Darius led her down a long passageway and then she heard the soft neighing of a horse.

Darius stopped by a box, released her hand and said, "This is Matrix's box. You have to be quiet, her baby may be sleeping. You have to lift me so I can see."

Tori complied, lifted him and peered into the box. A tall mare stood there, eyeing her with suspicion, but when the horse recognized Darius's voice, her expression immediately changed and she stepped closer, revealing the cutest foal Tamara had ever seen. Maybe it was the only foal she'd seen for real, but it was definitely cute.

The mare trotted over to where they stood, reaching out to be nuzzled by Darius, who squealed in delight.

"I haven't chosen a name for the baby yet," he said. "You can reach over and touch him. Matrix won't do anything."

Tori leaned over, reaching out to pet the foal. She looked up with watery, trusting eyes, and proceeded to lick Tori's hand.

Darius giggled. "She likes you," he said.

"I like her, too," Tori responded.

"Oh, well. You can put me down now, 'cause we have to go. I'm getting hungry. My mommy has been cooking all morning, so I'm sure we'll have something special. 'Bye, Matrix. 'Bye, baby, I'll get a name for you soon," he said, reaching over to touch them one last time.

When Tori put him down, he held her hand and they headed back to the house. Of course, with Darius chatting merrily to her and sometimes to himself.

When they entered the living room several minutes later, Carla turned to greet them.

"I hope he didn't exhaust you with all the chatter," she said.

"No, we had a fine time. He's adorable."

"We are going to eat shortly. Darius, go call your dad and uncle," Carla said, kissing him.

Without hesitation, Darius scampered from the room.

Carla turned to Tori. "I hope you're enjoying your stay here. Of course, Shayne and I have our tickets for the jazz festival's main event, so I'll finally get to hear you in person. I bought your album when I heard it was so good. I'm finally getting to meet you," she said, her smile soft and sincere.

"I'm glad you like the album. It was hard work, but it's what I've always wanted to do."

"Oh, I only have to see you singing on TV and I know you love your work. Come, we can go join the men in the dining room, but we girls will chat later. Tamara is bringing the baby over later this afternoon. She was supposed to be here already, but had an emergency."

"Oh, I'm sorry to hear. I hope it wasn't something serious," Tori asked.

"Oh, it's not Tamara. She's a vet and had emergency surgery with one of her patients."

"That's good. I'm looking forward to meeting her. Where is the baby?" Tori asked.

"She's upstairs sleeping. I just put her down

and she'll sleep for the next few hours. I love her, but it's an ongoing battle to get her to nap. Darius was the opposite, he slept all the time," Carla said.

"Russell told me he was born premature."

"Yes, that was a scary time for us, but we both loved him and I know that our presence in the hospital made him determined to live. Now Darius is a strong healthy boy. We call him our little miracle baby."

They walked down the hallway, coming to a stop at the entrance of a room filled with laughter.

Inside, the men—Shayne, Russell and Darius— were watching a game of cricket. They turned and smiled at the ladies and then turned back to the television.

"I'm going to have to force them away from the television so we can eat. It'll be pretty informal. I've set it out buffet-style so we'll just take our food and eat on the balcony outside and leave the men to the cricket.

"Gentlemen, you can go take what you want. Darius, I'll fix your plate. Shayne, please say the grace," Carla said.

Shayne thanked God for his family and then both he and Russell left the buffet table with plates brimming to capacity. Soon, they were sitting with their eyes glued to the TV. Carla and Tori headed outside with their own modestly filled plates.

When they were seated, Tori looked at all the

food she'd put on her plate. "I'm going to have to be careful, but I wanted to try everything."

"You may have taken a bit of everything, but your plate is nowhere close to being like Shayne's and Russell's. But you need to eat well. I'm sure that with all those engagements, you can't have time to take care of yourself," Carla said.

"No, I promise I'll take care of myself. And my manager makes sure I go to the gym for an hour each day and I have a nutritionist who makes sure I eat well," Tori replied.

"It must be good to be able to afford all those things." Carla said.

"Perhaps. It's good to have lots of money. Unfortunately, it doesn't always make you happy," she replied.

"But I'm sure you're happy," said Carla.

"Oh, I'm happy with my career. It's my love life that has me going crazy."

"Russell?" Carla asked.

"Yes, Russell. When I met him I was just singing in a club, but with all these changes going on in my life, I'm not even sure what to do."

"Oh, the conflict with your music and the time you have to spend with him…?"

"Yes, that and commitment. Ironically, when we got into this relationship we did discuss this, and we both agreed that we were focused on our work and commitment wasn't possible at that time. We didn't totally reject the notion of something long-term, but it was not to affect our career goals and aspirations," Tori replied.

"But now he wants more?"

"Yes, he wants more. I want more, too, but I don't want to give up my music. I've just started, and he wanted me to give it up. He didn't say that directly, but he wants children and a wife to come home to at nights. I can't be that kind of wife."

"And you're sure that's what he wants? For you to give up all you've worked so hard for? Seems rather selfish," Carla said.

"It does. That's made it so easy to say no and move on."

"Shayne was similar in many ways. It took him a while to care about lots of things. I call him a work in progress."

"Definitely, aren't they all?" Tori laughed, spreading her hands wide.

"Tori, I think I'm going to like you."

"That's great, sista. I definitely feel the same way."

"Tell me you love romance novels as much as Tamara and I do, and we'll be friends for life."

"I just love me some romance, so I'm sure we'll be friends for a long time."

"Wait until I tell Tamara. She'll have you and Russell down the aisle in no time." She started to laugh and stopped when she realized what she had said.

"It's okay. I may be a bit sensitive when it

comes to Russell and marriage, but I can still talk about it. You and Shayne seem to have a good marriage," Tori commented.

"We do have a good one. Doesn't mean we don't have our conflicts, but we made a vow that we'd never go to bed without resolving any quarrel we have. It's worked for us."

"Maybe Russell and I should start taking your advice."

Before Carla could respond, Russell came onto the balcony. "Tori, it's getting late. We have to head on back to the auditorium for the rehearsal."

She glanced down at the time. "I didn't realize it was so late."

"It's fine," he replied. "It won't take us more than fifteen minutes to get there."

Tori turned to Carla. "It was great to meet you. I hope I see you before I leave. I'm sorry Tamara didn't get here before I left."

"The same here. You enjoy your rehearsal."

"I will. I'm excited about singing on Sunday. Even if I don't get to see you before I leave, I promise to call."

She was surprised when Carla hugged her and gave her a kiss on her cheek.

"Shayne asked me to say goodbye for him. Darius fell asleep in his lap. I told him I'd pass on his goodbye."

Tori regretted having to leave so early, but she couldn't miss rehearsal. There was something about the family she liked and it made her realize how much she'd missed growing up in a family where love was the most important emotion.

For a while they drove in silence, enjoying the wind blowing through the windows. It was warm but the breeze offered a measure of comfort.

"Your family is nice," she said, breaking the silence.

"Yeah, of course, I'm the nicest."

"I'm not sure about that. Darius is a real charmer," she replied.

"Oh, he doesn't count. He's just a kid. He's naturally charming. Now, me, I've had to cultivate my skills to be charming."

"True, you can be charming at times," she teased.

"At times? And here I was thinking that I'm the epitome of charm."

"Sorry to burst your bubble."

"Oh, no worry. I know you're just talking. I've worked my charm on you and it worked."

"Aren't we a bit too confident?" she asked, laughing.

"And I'm sure the charm can still work magic," he replied, his tone implying a challenge.

"Is that so? I love your confidence, or should I say presumption?"

"A man has to be confident when he goes after what he wants. If he doesn't, he's less of a man."

"Spoken like a true man."

"Definitely. A man you want, but are not willing to admit it."

"Not willing to admit. I do want you. So who's not willing to admit it? It's not the wanting that worries me. It's what's left after the wanting."

"What's left?"

"The nothingness."

"You think that all we have for each other is the sex? That's what you think I want from you?"

She didn't answer.

"What can I do to prove to you that what I feel is more than sex?" he asked.

Again she didn't reply.

"I know what. When the concert is over, stay behind for a week and let me show you. We'll get to know each other. No sex, no touching, just getting to know each other."

"I'm not sure I can get away for a whole week?"

"But you can ask. Tell them you like Barbados. They're filming your video here right after. You can tell them you're tired and need some rest. We need this time."

Tori hesitated before she replied. "Okay, I'll see what I can do. But I won't make you any promises," she said.

"That's fine with me."

The rest of the ride was completed in silence. When they arrived at the auditorium, Tori immediately jumped from the car, heading in the direction of the performers' entrance.

He followed her slowly. If that was how she wanted to be, then let her. He'd learn to deal with her moods. He wasn't perfect so he couldn't expect her to be.

Inside he was still feeling on top of the world. She agreed to stay behind. He'd show her Barbados and maybe, just maybe the magic of the island would show her that love was more important than anything else.

Later in the auditorium, he watched her, the consummate performer.

He had no doubt that on the weekend, she would enchant the audience and have them eating out of her hands. Tori's performance was not only about the singing, but was also her ability to communicate her passion to the audience.

It was that quality that had attracted him to her. On reflection, he might have fallen in love with her that night when he'd seen her sing for the first time. Yes, he'd been turned on by her sexy, sultry look, but even then her personality had radiated around the room.

When he finally met her, it was that same personality that had made his love for her grow.

As she continued to rehearse, he stood and left. The emotions that raged inside him were a bit too much to handle. He'd never felt like this before and he felt vulnerable and scared.

Her people were here so she didn't need him.

Hours later, Russell sat staring out to sea. Years

ago, he'd come here with his friends to swim. The beach had changed a bit. With the constant fluctuation of the tides, the large expanse of natural beach no longer existed. People had discovered their secret place. A few lifeguard huts dotted the almost mile-long beach.

But the essentials were still there. The pure white sand glistened and the sun tossed its rays in shades of red and yellow and orange across the water.

He hadn't come here to think about the chaos that was his life. He just wanted to feel close to his creator. Ironically, he'd failed to talk to God during the past few years. He'd been too caught up with being macho and living up to his reputation as a womanizer to deal with his soul.

Maybe he'd needed to come home at this time to remember the things that had made him the person he was. He deserved the tongue-lashing he'd received from Gladys. She had read him his first Bible story and taught him the difference between right and wrong.

He had no excuse and he was making none.

When the sun gave him its final wink before disappearing, he allowed himself one moment of vulnerability.

He allowed tears, soothing and comforting, to trickle down his cheeks as he acknowledged who he was.

Tomorrow would be another day.

He did leave with one clear resolve. He would make things right with Tori.

He loved her and thanked God for bringing her into his life.

Tori sang the final note and placed the cordless microphone on the stand. Good, rehearsals were over and she could relax until the concert.

Her gaze scanned the auditorium, but she couldn't see Russell anywhere.

He'd left.

Or maybe he was on the outside looking for her to come out.

Waving goodbye to the team, she hurried outside and realized immediately that his car was gone.

Silly. She'd made no arrangement to go with him. In fact, she'd given him no indication that she wanted to be with him. So his interpretation was by no means incorrect.

At the time, she'd scolded herself for thinking about staying on after the festival was done.

The thought of spending time with Russell was appealing. But what good would it do? It would bring them closer, but nothing else would change.

There was no life for the two of them. They lived in two totally different worlds.

But maybe, just maybe, they could make it work. It was that glimmer of possibility that made her consider staying behind. She had no doubt they would end up in bed, but she did not want that to be the overriding factor.

Whatever they hoped for had to go beyond that; beyond the bare physical.

On the drive to the hotel, she really started to see the island. It was indeed beautiful and even in the fading light, she appreciated it for the first time. Her arrival here and the hectic nature of the upcoming concert had forced her to block everything else from her mind.

Now that she could relax, she was able to observe more. Maybe staying behind wouldn't be so bad after all. She'd get a chance to see the island and the beauty she'd heard about.

Island girl Rihanna always spoke of her island home, and Tori could see now why the young singer always returned home when she needed to recuperate.

The island's magic was already working its spell.

At the hotel, she took a long shower, washing the stress of the day away.

Dressing quickly, she made her way to Russell's room. When she knocked, he almost immediately opened the door.

Only her self-discipline stopped her from jumping on him immediately.

He wore a towel, low on his hips.

How she loved his body. His chest was covered with hair, soft hair, which disappeared below the edge of the towel.

Already she could see his arousal.

She closed the door behind her before she reached out and loosened the towel, letting it fall to the floor.

She placed her hand on his chest, pressing him backward until the bed stopped him and she pushed him gently down.

She lowered herself immediately, taking his penis in her hands, enjoying its length and hardness.

Tori stroked him gently, their eyes locked in a knowing gaze. His eyes blazed as she knew the pleasure she gave.

Removing her hands, she bent her head and took him in her mouth, careful not to hurt him with her teeth.

She loved his taste and scent. The freshness of his shower gel. His manliness.

For a while she pleasured him, loving the way he groaned and moaned, his face registering his intense pleasure.

"Come, stop," he eventually said. "I want to feel myself inside you."

She joined him, allowing him to place her on her back.

"Take your clothes off," he commanded.

She obeyed, taking them off slowly to tantalize him with her seductive striptease.

Her T-shirt and jeans off, he rose briefly to draw her to him. He remained on his back, indicating that she should sit on him.

She complied, positioned herself over him and

lowered herself slowly onto his erection. She watched him as he entered her, his eyes closed, his face in a grimace of pleasure.

When he was completely inside her until she could feel every ridge and muscle, every inch of him, he raised his hips slamming into her with a force that left her breathless.

Somehow she knew this ride wouldn't be an easy one, but she didn't want it to be. She wanted to ride him hard and fast, in the hope that this moment would purge her of her intense need for him.

And the ride was wild. With each downward movement, Russell met her with a stroke that had both of them screaming with the intensity of their coupling.

She knew it would be over soon; felt the coming stir of the climax. She did not slow her pace but egged him on with words of passion that turned her on until she thought she would not get enough of him.

When the ride came to an end, Tori collapsed on Russell, feeling the sharp spasms deep inside her as he groaned with the intensity of his release.

As they lay holding each other, their bodies shook with their passion.

Exhausted, they both fell asleep.

In the early hours of the morning, Tori woke to find herself alone in bed. She stretched, feeling the soreness in her body, but feeling very much alive.

Russell stood naked by the window. Even in the shadows of the lights from outside, the beauty of his body stirred her.

She rose, walking quietly across the soft carpet. When she reached him, he turned, placing her to stand in front of him, and then enclosing her in his embrace.

No words transpired between them, but they needed none.

Soon, the sun made its appearance, smiling at them from behind a dull gray cloud, while transforming the sky into shades of the palest blue.

For the first time, Russell watched the sun rise and he wasn't alone.

Chapter 11

The next few days passed in a flurry of activity. Both concerts played to capacity crowds and Tori left each one knowing that the audience had enjoyed her performance. The final night of the festival she'd received a standing ovation.

The video shoot, too, had gone exceptionally well and the technical personnel seemed pleased with the footage they'd taken.

Tori watched as a plane passed overhead, on its way from the island. She wished she could fly after it and jump on, but she knew that would make no difference to what was going on in her life. She'd made the right decision. She needed this time with Russell to decide what she wanted out of their relationship.

Despite everything she'd tried, Russell Knight disturbed her every thought.

She left the window open, preferring the warmth of the tropical breeze.

When she glanced at her watch, she realized that the time was near. In a few minutes, Russell would be knocking at the door and she'd be off to spend the day with him.

She had no idea what he had in store, but he'd promised her she would see some of the island. She was glad she made seeing the island a requirement of their stay.

She turned and glanced at herself in the mirror for the fiftieth time. She looked good, definitely good.

Russell would like what she wore, a pale yellow tube top and a pair of her jeans that clung to every curve of her body.

The doorbell buzzed and her heartbeat immediately quickened.

Russell.

She raced to the door, stopping abruptly when she reached it and taking a quick glance again in the mirror.

Did her butt look a bit too big? Maybe she shouldn't have worn the jeans.

No, she needed to take control. She was paying her gym a lot to keep her looking fit and good. She had nothing to be worried about.

When the doorbell buzzed again, she took a deep breath, opened the door and made sure her brightest smile was in place.

Russell bent his head and captured her lips in a hungry kiss.

Tori returned it, enjoying the feel of him next to her.

When she pulled away, he smiled and said, "Sorry, I couldn't resist. I wanted to see if that lipstick you're wearing tastes like cherries."

"And does it?" she asked.

"Definitely," he replied, smiling when she blushed. "You're ready?" he asked.

"I'm ready. I'm looking forward to seeing some of your lovely island."

"Then you're in for a treat," he said, taking her hand in his.

He turned to go and she followed, closing the door behind her.

They walked slowly down the stairs. No words were needed; they were both content to hold each other's hand.

A few minutes later, Russell's car was pulling out into the highway.

For a while they traveled along the highway, slowing down at points where it was being repaired.

They took a left turn and followed a narrow road that led away from the suburbs.

Soon, tall sugarcane plants flanked the road that took them farther and farther away from the city.

Occasionally, the sugarcane fields gave way to tiny villages, where young men watched with curiosity as the car passed by.

In the distance, low hills, lush with vegetation, beckoned them.

"Where are we?" she asked, her voice sounding awed. "It's so different from the area where the hotel is. I must get some photos but I forgot to bring my camera."

"I brought one, so you can use it. It's in the backseat."

"Oh, thanks. I really wouldn't have wanted to miss putting this on film."

"It's the beauty of the island I miss most."

"So why did you leave if you love the island so much?" she asked.

He glanced across at her. "Sometimes I'm not even sure, but at that time, I wanted my independence and I didn't believe I could get it here. Along with that I've always been fascinated by the bright lights of New York. Who doesn't love New York?" he asked.

"I understand what you mean. As soon as I left college I headed straight there. I wanted to sing and New York was the place to be."

"Well, it has all paid off for you. You're achieving all you've wanted."

He slowed the car when he turned a corner. A little boy was leading a flock of brown and black sheep across the road.

"You know you're in Barbados when you see black belly sheep. I had my own when I was young and had to take care of it. Shayne wanted to teach us responsibility. Tamara eventually took care of mine and hers. I think that's when she realized she wanted to be a vet."

"You didn't like that kind of responsibility much, did you?"

"If not for Tamara, the poor animal would have died. I was too busy studying and doing other things to remember it. Tamara took over without hesitation. And that started years of stray animals parading through our house," Russell said.

"How long has she been a vet?" Tori asked.

"About three years, but she's only working part-time right now. She has two babies to take care of."

"Of course, it's in the genes. I'm sure you'll probably have a set of twins someday too," she said.

"Oh, I intend to. I want lots of kids."

Another thing they didn't have in common. She wasn't sure if she wanted any kids.

"You're quiet," Russell observed. "You don't want children."

"I haven't really thought about it," she lied. She had thought about it. Often. But she wasn't sure if she'd make a good mother. Her parents hadn't been the best and she really didn't want to be like them.

"I think you'd make a good mother," he said.

"Maybe. Unfortunately, not at this time. I'm too focused on my career to think of marriage or children." She stopped immediately, knowing she'd said something she shouldn't have.

"I'm sorry," she whispered.

"It's okay. I asked. A lot has happened in the year since we parted ways. I have no doubt how you feel about your career."

"It may be better if we change the subject."

"We're almost at the place I want you to see. It's Mount Hillaby, the highest point in the island. Not a mountain in the true sense of the word, but one of the most beautiful places on the island."

He slowed the car, parking it under the shade of a tall, well-canopied tree.

When he turned the engine off she stepped out, knowing that he'd do the gentlemanly thing and come to open her door.

She headed for a wooden bench a few feet up, climbing quickly.

Russell followed her.

On reaching the top, they stood, unable to say anything. Spread before her was the island at its most beautiful and she lamented that it was not sunrise. She looked toward the east of the island. The sun was already overhead, its heat warming her bare arms.

What was beautiful about the island were the wonderful shades of green and gold. In the distance, the Atlantic Ocean beat against the rocks and cliffs that seemed to be a prominent part of the island's east coast.

She could see the occasional cluster of houses, partially hidden in a valley.

"Take this," he said, handing her the camera. "You can have the photos you want."

"Thanks. The island is so beautiful."

"It is, isn't it?"

"I can now see why you ache to come home. I could live here. Even though I've been rehearsing, I can tell the pace of life is slower. Definitely different from the U.S."

"That's what I hated about it. Everyone seemed to be wasting their lives. It was only when I was in the U.S. for a few months that I realized that most of what I'd grown to hate about the island is what I missed most. I didn't go to the beach often, but all of a sudden I found myself missing the warmth of the ocean."

"Can we go in the water sometime today?" she asked.

"Yeah, sure. I've been thinking about it. We can go when we get back to the hotel. You're still willing to stay at the plantation for the next two weeks?"

"As long as your brother and his wife don't mind."

"Shayne and Carla have already said it's fine. And Darius is excited to have the famous singer he sees on television in his home. He'll soon be asking you to go to his school."

She grimaced.

"No need to look like that. You can turn him down with a smile."

"If he asks, I'll think about it. It's just all those children," she said.

"You stand in front of adults and sing and a few tiny tots have you all scared."

She had to laugh. What he said was so true. She wasn't comfortable around children. "Okay, I'll promise right here and now that if Darius asks I'll do it."

"That's my girl. And on that note, I think we need to get going. We have lunch reservations in an hour at the Crane Hotel, one of the best all-inclusive hotels on the island."

He reached for her hand, a habit she was growing accustomed to. When they got to the car, he released her and she felt a strange emptiness.

"Music?" he asked.

"Yeah," she replied. "Just not my own."

"Okay, what about Alicia Keys? Shayne has the new one in the player."

"Yeah, I love her music. Definitely put it on."

Tori joined in when Alicia's latest single started. And then Russell added his rather off-key tenor.

Tori thought she'd never seen Russell look happier.

The quiet strum of a folk guitar tickled the senses, bringing images of dancing women and happy children.

The meal had been good, a dish of flying fish and creamed breadfruit. Tori had eaten the local delicacy like a native.

Of course, she'd chosen the restaurant's special for dessert, a decadent cheesecake, topped with local golden apples instead of the cherries or strawberries she was accustomed to.

Feeling tired, they decided to lounge on the beach for the rest of the afternoon with a chilled bottle of wine. The sea on this side was not the best for swimming. There were other days they could get to the beach.

Waves crashed against the cliff in the distance while a tiny calm pool of water beckoned them with its coolness. Though her body felt tired, Tori found it difficult to drift off to sleep. Tired from driving all day, Russell had fallen asleep in no time.

In sleep, he seemed gentler. This was not the first time she had seen him like this, but it felt strange this time. She could not keep her eyes off him. His body rippled with tone and muscles. Her hands ached to touch him.

She loved the feel of his body under her hand and was still fascinated that she loved to feel his firmness beneath her.

His body shifted and Russell turned toward her, his breathing steady.

She needed to move. She could spend all day staring at him, but she needed a time-out. She rose, feeling like a child about to go on a short journey.

She wanted to explore and she skipped happily along the sand.

Between her toes, the sand squelched and she knelt on the ground, pulling sand toward her as she began to dig a hole.

Soon her sand castle started to take shape and her mind conjured up images of men ready for battle and damsels in distress. But in her fantasy, a single woman stood looking out to sea, waiting for her knight in shining armor to come.

And the knight in her castle bore a startling resemblance to Russell. Well, he was a Knight indeed. One to come save her from the jaws of the evil dragon.

Her castle started to take shape. She'd never built a sand castle before. Instinct told her what she needed to do to make it right.

She heard the sound of footsteps crunching in the sand and turned to see Russell heading in her direction.

When he reached her he didn't say anything. Instead he lowered himself to the ground, kneeling to join her.

For a while they worked in silence, the squelching of sand the only sound.

Russell added the walls that surrounded the castle and built a moat to protect the structure from the incoming waves.

By the time they were done, they'd created a large and elaborate structure.

"We work well together, don't we?" he asked.

"Yes," she replied. It did feel strange. This easy camaraderie between them.

"You ready to go?" he asked. "The water is coming in. Our hard work will soon be gone."

"It's sad that something that took so long to build could so easily be destroyed."

"I know," he said, grabbing her arm.

"Come, let's go. I can't bear to see it gone. Race me to the end of the beach," she said.

"Okay, you're on. Remember, I took track in school."

"I did, too." And before he could respond she was off at breakneck speed.

Russell ran behind her, easily passing her, and lay on the sand when she reached him.

"I may have won, but I don't know what craziness I got myself into. I'm beat. I can't get up from here. Help me," he requested.

When Tori reached her hand out to help him up, he pulled her down on top of him. His arms held her tight as she struggled to get away, her laughter echoing across the beach.

When his lips touched hers, she responded instinctively, returning the kiss with an abandonment that surprised even her. It was as if some part of her wanted desperately to need him. And she did need him.

As she kissed him back, the emptiness she'd felt for so long lifted, leaving a joy deep inside that started to bubble. And as she responded to his touch it was not a groan of pleasure, but the sound of laughter that came from deep within.

Unexpectedly Russell started to laugh, too. Tori was sure that the others on the beach thought they were crazy, but she really didn't care.

She just wanted to treasure the moment before the harsh realities of life turned all she was feeling into a dream.

The next few days were idyllic and special, but thoughts of returning to New York were ever present. It was not that either of them wanted it, but the reality of the U.S. and Tori's job hung like a shadow over them.

Russell sighed with the tension of pent-up frustrations. In two days, Tori would return to her glamorous life and he'd return to the newspaper.

The thought saddened him. To make himself feel better, he decided to go riding. He ended up thinking about his and Tori's situation even more. He'd hoped that their time together would be longer, but soon they'd be making their way back home.

His respect for her had grown by measures. She'd told him a lot about her work and all she'd experienced in the past year.

Russell realized that a lot of his ideas about women and their role came from his brother's own beliefs.

Shayne believed that women should stay home and take care of their children.

Of course, his marriage to Carla had put him right.

He, too, had to undergo a serious change of attitude.

Ironically, Russell had never seen himself as macho, but Tori had showed him areas he needed to work on and he'd given in willingly.

Of course now he realized that there was a joy in being equal partners in all areas of the relationship.

He wanted that and more with Tori. He wanted to wake up each morning and find Tori lying next to him. He wanted to see her stomach swell with the weight of a child.

He urged the horse on, loving the feel of the cool morning breeze against his face. His parents had loved horses and riding, and like Shayne and Tamara, he'd learned to ride early. However, he did not share their desire to ride whenever he could. Yes, he enjoyed riding, but an occasional ride was enough for him.

He rode from the house, exploring the still familiar place, which brought back childhood memories of him and Tamara romping through the bushes.

Letting the reins out, he broke into a gallop. The speed exhilarated him. He almost gave a loud shout of delight when he noticed another horse and rider in the distance.

At the sound of his approach, the rider slowed, turned around and waited.

It was Shayne.

Maybe this was time to make peace.

When he reached his brother, Russell gently reined the horse in. He watched as his brother dismounted and he eventually followed suit.

"So, you and Tori having a good time?" Shayne asked.

"Yes, we are. Thanks for allowing her to stay at the house."

"The house is still your home. Any friend of yours is welcome. You know that." Shayne moved toward the shade of a large tree.

"Yes, I know," Russell replied as he joined his brother.

"I like her. Carla likes her, too. Carla is a good judge of character. I hope you're dealing with whatever needs to be worked out. Even Darius loves her and he's all excited because he's teaching her how to ride."

"This week has been good for us. I'm not sure how much has been resolved, but we've taken a step in the right direction."

"Don't want to be inquisitive, but why are the two of you not married? Anyone can see that you're in love with each other."

"It's that obvious?" Russell asked.

"Yes, I keep waiting for the two of you to pounce

on each other right there on the dining room table."
Shayne laughed.

"Now, that would shock Gladys right to her room."

"Gladys has caught Carla and me in a few risqué situations before. She just cleared her throat and walked away. Didn't even blush the next time she saw us." Shayne's laughter echoed in the silence.

"Lord, I'd have been so embarrassed."

"Oh, we were. Since then we've tried to be careful where we end up making love. Don't want these intrusions too often."

"I can bet. Tori and I…" Russell paused.

"Oh, so you and the celebrity are doing the dirty."

Russell didn't know it was possible, but heat washed across his face. "Yes, we're normal, aren't we?"

"Which means things are going a bit better than I thought," Shayne replied. "That's good."

"We're definitely working on it."

"So, what happened between the two of you? If you don't mind me asking."

"When I met Tori she was still singing in a club. She was waiting on her dream to come true. When she got the contract, I, being all macho and stuff, thought that she'd marry me and give up the music."

When he saw the look on his brother's face, he said, "Yes, yes, I know. Silly me, right?"

"Boy, don't you watch TV, read books? Women never ever want you to respond like that. You were going crazy. No one, especially women, likes to be ruled," Shayne said.

"I learned that the hard way. Coming to Barbados was the first time I've seen her in a year."

"She must have been surprised when you turned up," Shayne said.

"Yeah, she was definitely surprised. But it's been okay. I know she still has feelings for me. We've been doing the 'dirty,' as you say, but it's been good. But she'll be soon going back to her glamorous celebrity life."

"And you're going to let her go?" Shayne asked.

"Yes, I have to let her go."

"I don't mean like that. Are you going to let her just walk out of your life without discussing the future? You love the woman?" Shayne asked.

When Russell nodded, he added, "Then show it."

For a while they sat in silence, the only sound the rustling of the wind in the trees.

"So, we okay?" Shayne said.

"We okay, bro," Russell replied.

Strangely enough, he thought the two of them would have a long profound conversation. Instead, all that he'd planned to say had been summed up in those single words from his brother.

"You want to race?" Russell asked.

"I was wondering when you'd ask," Shayne replied. "You ready?"

"Yeah, whenever you are."

"Good, let's see who gets back to the plantation house first," his brother said, jumping to his feet.

Before Russell could stand, Shayne had already mounted his horse, and was off.

Adrenaline pumping, he quickly mounted and charged after Shayne. The race would be a good one. His brother loved horses, but Russell was the one who had the speed.

He had every intention of winning.

Chapter 12

Tori stepped into the kitchen wondering if Carla was there, but the aroma of breakfast forced her to shed her apprehension and walk in.

"Tori, morning," Carla greeted. "What do you want for breakfast?"

"You sure you want me to answer that question? I have a healthy appetite."

"Well, I'm doing scrambled eggs and bacon with lots of toast."

"That's perfect. Add a cup of coffee and I'm your friend for life."

"Now, that's my kind of girl. I can't get my day started without a cup of good Blue Mountain coffee. I can't understand this obsession with tea."

"I've heard so much about Jamaican coffee, I can't wait to taste it."

"Well, you sit yourself down and we'll eat a hearty breakfast and chitchat," Carla said, indicating a chair at the table."

"Let me help," Tori said.

"Let's make a deal. This is your first visit in my home, so I must play hostess. After our breakfast and our little girly chat, we'll be the best of friends. So tomorrow, we'll make breakfast together. I'm always here to make breakfast at seven. Shayne will leave a little after eight o'clock."

"And Darius?" Tori asked.

"Oh, he'll soon be down asking about his cereal. He's into Froot Loops and Corn Pops. Won't eat anything else."

"He's a sweetheart. How old is he now?"

"He'll soon be seven. He was born premature at twenty-six weeks. He was the one who brought Shayne and me together."

"And he's so big now?"

"Yeah, people have the misconception that preemies remain small. Darius is proof that they don't. And to think that we could have lost him."

There was a noise in the hallway and the staccato of footsteps. Seconds later, Darius raced into the room.

He stopped when he saw them sitting there. Like the perfect gentleman he walked over to Tori, a broad smile on his face.

"Hi, Auntie Tori, hope you slept well?"

"I did, honey," she replied, hugging him.

"I'm going to eat some cereal now. You want some of my Froot Loops?"

"Thanks, but I'll let you have all your cereal. Maybe another morning."

"Okay, Mommy, where's Daddy and Uncle Russell? They're not in their room."

"I know your dad went riding, but I'm not sure about Russell." Carla turned to Tori, who shook her head in response. She thought he was still sleeping.

Breakfast passed with most of the conversation controlled by Darius. When he was finished, he left, announcing that he was going to watch *Sesame Street*.

As he walked away, Tori could not help her comment. "I hope one day I have a son just like him."

"Maybe you will. The Knights have a strong family resemblance," Carla said, a knowing smile on her face.

"I'm not sure about that. But Russell and I are trying to work things out."

"You've known him a long time?"

"More than a year. I was singing in a club when he came and introduced himself. He was charming and the perfect gentleman. Sexy, too."

"The Knight men have a way of being like that. Sexy? Definitely. Stubborn? Without a doubt."

"Yes, Russell is definitely stubborn. If he wasn't we'd probably be apart right now."

"So you were friends, broke up and now you're friends again."

"Something like that. It's a bit more complex. Just say my new career made me lose the man I love. I'm hoping I can earn his love again. When he asked me to marry him last year, I refused. He wanted me to give up my career and marry him."

"Sounds like another man I know. Shayne wasn't too happy when I said I wanted to go back to work, but he has still been very supportive. I opened a travel agency here. I have a few in the U.S., but they're run by the managers there. Thanks to technology and the Internet. My best friend, Sandra, runs the head office in Virginia."

"Girl, what I wouldn't do for a career like that! But I love what I do and I can't imagine not singing."

"You'd want to have an ordinary job just like mine?" Carla asked.

"Ordinary? There isn't anything ordinary about what you're doing. I know you travel agents get to travel to all sorts of exotic places."

"And so do you. But you're right. I love to travel. That's how I came to Barbados and met Shayne."

"You did. Island romance?"

"I'm not sure if I'd call it that. But I came here to the opening of a Hilton Hotel a few years ago. Met Shayne and it was instant attraction. Enough to say we ended up spending most of my week here in bed and the rest is history. Our start definitely wasn't a good one. But eventually, it all worked itself out. We fell in love and got married."

"How romantic! Sounds like a story from one of my romance novels."

Carla was definitely not what Tori had expected, but it sure made being here in Barbados lots of fun.

Russell and Shayne found them when they arrived back at the house. The ride had left them feeling ravenous and they devoured their breakfast.

"So, did you and Russell have a good race?" Carla asked.

"I did notice that Shayne looked a bit harried and Russell has a smug smile on his lips. Whipped you, did he?" she asked her husband.

"Yeah, but he was on the better horse. And when I met him, I'd been riding for a whole hour already. His horse wasn't even tired."

"Yeah, yeah, sore loser."

Their first week in Barbados went quickly, but Russell still felt a distance between himself and the woman he loved.

As he typed on his laptop his amazement at what Tori had accomplished increased his respect for her and her craft. He'd not even realized she had written some of the songs on her bestselling album.

He'd discovered a lot about her. She had a brother, and her mother and father still lived in Reading, a small town a few hours from New York.

She'd left Reading at age eighteen to move to New York, where she played the piano with several music companies, but she'd given up the classical music. She wanted to sing jazz and R & B.

He did discover that she'd not been home to her family in years. He wondered why, even though he could speculate about the answer, but he knew without proper research a journalist could find himself in trouble.

He heard footsteps and looked up to see Carla standing watching him.

"You're so much like Shayne and neither of you knows how much pain you're causing each other."

He continued to stare at her.

"I'm sorry. I didn't mean to say that. Shayne always tells me I should think before I say what's on my mind, but as you see I've not been too successful," she said.

"I can sympathize with you. I'm not one for hypocrisy, so I know what it's like to speak your mind. Of course, I have to be more disciplined on the job, but it doesn't often work."

She glanced at the picture on the computer's desktop and then turned to him. "I can see you love her. And she knows."

"So, why do I feel like I'm fighting a losing battle? That even though we've worked out so much, there's still this large wall between us?"

"Since you've been reading your note on her history, you should have some ideas of what's wrong. Why do you macho men always have to believe that it's always about you? You should see the way she looks at you when she thinks no one is watching. She definitely is in love."

"But what can I do? I want to marry her, have kids and settle down here."

"Well, Shayne will be glad to hear you say that, but you need to give Tori time. She's just settled into a new career and in time she'll know how to deal with everything, including you. You just need to be patient."

He could tell that his look of frustration did not surprise her.

"You know something? I'm amazed at how similar you and Shayne are. He's stubborn, loves to get his own way...and he has the Knight complex," she said.

"The Knight complex?" he asked, a look of confusion on his face.

"Yes, you're like knights of old. There were brave men, but they felt that they always had to be in control of the people around them and the people of the city."

"And how does that relate to me?" he asked, though he knew exactly what she meant.

"That's the same response I'd expect from Shayne. So I'll leave you here. I hear my daughter calling me. Russell, I can only say I wish you luck. To be honest, you're a Knight and you're too much like my husband not to come to your senses before it's too late."

She reached up on her tiptoes and kissed him on the cheek.

"Have a good night, Russell Knight. Sweet dreams," she said.

Russell watched her as she walked away, only to break into laughter when she turned the corner.

He hoped he came to his senses soon.

Russell closed the latest edition of his newspaper, which he'd purchased in the local bookstore, and wondered if Tori planned to go riding with them again today. She was a quick learner and seemed to enjoy having Darius with them on their rides.

He rose from the bed and headed to the bathroom. He showered quickly and then donned his usual T-shirt, jeans and a pair of riding boots.

Downstairs, minutes later, he grabbed a bunch of grapes and an orange and waited.

As expected the next person came downstairs with the crashing of footsteps.

Darius raced into the kitchen and came to an abrupt stop when he saw his uncle sitting and eating.

"Good morning, Uncle Russell, I thought you'd gone and left me."

"Do you think I would have gone and left my favorite nephew?" Russell asked.

"Of course not, Uncle Russell," Darius replied.

"Good, what do you want for breakfast?"

Darius glanced at what was in his uncle's hands. "Just some grapes and an orange," he finally said.

"No cereal this morning?" Russell tried not to laugh.

"No, it's a lot better to ride after a healthy breakfast of fruit."

"That's fine, Darius, but there's nothing wrong with eating cereal for breakfast."

"So I can still have my cereal?" Darius asked, his gaze on the cupboard where his mother stored the cereal.

When Russell nodded, Darius jumped up and down. "Can I have Froot Loops?"

"No problem. Where are the bowls?" he asked.

"In that cupboard there," Darius said, pointing at the cupboard where Russell was standing.

Several minutes later, while Darius was eating, Tori walked in. "I'm sorry. I overslept. I wanted to be outside before the sun came up. Darius, you beat me to it."

"Yes, I did. Mom woke me up, helped me to get dressed and went back to sleep. She says that Lynn-Marie kept her up all night. She was cranky, but she's only a baby."

"Okay, let me just have a glass of juice and we can be on the road. I can't wait to get on Gemini."

"Oh, she loves you."

"Well, is everyone ignoring me?" Russell finally said.

Both Tori and Darius turned to him and laughed.

"Sorry, Uncle Russell. Auntie and I were chatting. We won't forget you again."

"I'd suggest that if we want to get a ride in before the sun is completely up, we need to get moving."

"I'm done with my cereal. We can leave now! Hooray!" Darius shouted with excitement.

"I'll wash the things in the sink while the two of you get the horses ready," Russell said.

Before he could finish the sentence Tori and Darius were gone.

He cleared the table and quickly washed everything in the sink, all the while humming to Tori's current single. He'd created a monster and Darius had helped. The past few days had been perfect. Having Darius around had made them keep their passions in check. Instead, they'd just enjoyed being in each other's company.

His task completed, he dried his hands and headed for the stables where he knew Tori and Darius would be waiting impatiently.

As he expected, when he appeared, Darius shouted, "Come, come, let's go."

Five minutes later, they were riding down the trail they usually took before they reached the large pasture where Russell could let the horse gallop. Though a more than competent rider, Darius was only allowed to canter briskly so he remained with Tori while she tried to improve her skills on the horse.

Russell came to a stop and turned to watch them from afar.

Tori was good with Darius, proof that she'd make a good mother. This side of her came as a surprise to him. He'd never expected her to take so easily to Darius. Now he could imagine her with her stomach swollen with his child, or should he say children, as Tamara had proven that twins were a strong possibility?

He dismounted, moving to sit under a large mahogany tree on the fringe of the pasture. He tested the makeshift bench under the tree before he sat. He looked across the St. Thomas Valley. The sun had risen above the horizon, its rays already beginning to warm the land, but the occasional breeze still cooled the air.

He heard the rumbling of horses and turned to see Darius and Tori coming in his direction.

"It's time we head back home," he told them. "I have to go into the city on important business later this morning. Darius, I want you to take care of Tori for me."

"No problem, I'll take care of her. We can play video games or watch television."

"Thanks, I knew I could depend on you. I hope it's fine with you, Tori?" he asked.

"Of course it's fine. Darius and I have lots of fun."

Darius beamed. "See, I told you it's no problem."

"Well, that's good. Let's go."

He mounted the horse and followed them from a distance. He couldn't believe he was feeling a little bit jealous of the comfortable camaraderie Darius shared with Tori.

Despite their truce, and the fact that they enjoyed each other's company, the sexual tension still simmered beneath the surface.

But he was glad they'd spent the time together without physical contact. He'd proven to her that they could be together as friends.

One thing that he did realize about their relationship was that it was special and they only had to work at it; that to make it work they had to learn to respect each other. He'd failed in that area, but he was determined to rectify the situation.

When they arrived back at the stables, he offered to take care of the horses.

As Darius and Tori left, they turned and waved at him.

He continued to watch them.

Would he ever claim a woman and child as his own?

Tori walked slowly up the stairs to her room. Darius had fallen asleep while they were watching *Shrek* which he seemed to know by heart.

She was entering her room, intent on getting a bit of rest, when her cell phone rang.

It took a while before she located it in one of her bags. She'd not used it in the past few days.

It was her agent.

"Tori, I'm sorry to call, but I need you back in New York as soon as possible. You have an important meeting back here. Since your first album is doing so well, RIC Records wants to sign you to a multi-album contract. They want to move on it as soon as possible. In fact, they want a meeting in two days."

"Do I definitely have to be there?" She dreaded the response, but she knew what was coming.

"Are you crazy, girl? Of course you have to be here. The press has been invited. You have no choice. I've already booked a flight for you. It leaves at seven o'clock tomorrow morning, so please don't miss it."

Her agent knew her so well. She'd actually contemplated missing it. "I'll be on the flight."

When she put the phone down a few minutes later, she sat on the bed, unable to do anything. She could already imagine how Russell would react.

Though the past two weeks had been great and they'd made a step in the right direction, she knew that this would only take them two steps backward. She could only hope that Russell would understand, but she knew him too well.

She needed to let Carla know she'd be leaving, but she could do that later. Everyone was resting.

Instead of sitting while she waited, she decided to pack. It would make things easier.

While she was packing she heard a car in the distance. Russell must have returned.

She exited the room, quickly taking the stairs, and came to a halt when she saw Russell standing at the bottom. He smiled when he saw her, a smile that slowly changed to concern.

"What's wrong, Tori?" he asked.

"I have to go," she said. "I'm really sorry, but I have to go."

"When do you leave?"

She could already hear the wall being built. He was shutting her out. "In the morning. My flight leaves at seven o'clock."

"No problem. I'll take you. I'll wake early. You'll have to be at the airport by five thirty. I need to go up to my room and take a shower. I'll talk to you later."

Before she could respond, he turned and ran up the stairs, taking two or three at a time. When he reached the top, she expected him to turn around, but he only continued to his room.

She bowed her head, realizing that all they'd worked to accomplish had just been flushed down the drain.

Again, Russell had allowed his anger to get the better of him. He'd not ranted and raved, but he'd deliberately locked her out. Selfish bastard that he

was. He hadn't even asked her why she was returning to New York, but he was sure his assumption
was correct.

   He'd seen the guilt in her eyes and knew that it
had something to do with her work. Only time
would tell, but now he really didn't want to hear.

Chapter 13

Tori's return to New York had not been a totally happy one. Though the conflict between her and Russell had been somewhat resolved, she was still unsure about the direction of her life and her relationship with him. There was no doubt about that. But did she love him enough to give up her freedom?

Their time in Barbados had drawn them closer, but she knew that his reaction to her sudden departure served to emphasize his true feelings about her career.

When the phone rang, she immediately glanced over at the clock. 5:30 a.m.

Who on earth could be calling her so early in the morning?

Her mother's name showed up on the display.

"Hello, Mom," she greeted. "What's wrong?"

Her mother didn't answer immediately, and when she did she avoided the question.

"Tori, you're back from Barbados?" she asked.

"Yes, Mom. I came back a few days ago. You're okay, Mom?"

"I'm fine. I saw a news report about the festival on one of the entertainment channels. Everyone is saying that you were good, really good."

"Thanks, Mom. I enjoyed doing it. And Barbados, it's a beautiful country."

"I know. That's where your father and I went for our honeymoon. But I'm sure it has changed a lot over the years."

"Oh, it has changed. It's a very modern country. It has been able to blend a sense of the past with all the technology of the future."

"That's good. I know that so many countries fail to hold on to their past."

"It hasn't been easy, but some still revere the culture of the past. Fortunately, elements of that culture were well integrated into the festival I took part in."

"I'm glad you were able to enjoy it and it wasn't all work," her mother responded.

"How's Jake doing? Has he finished med school yet?"

She heard the surprise in her mother's voice. Tori never asked about her brother.

"Yes, he's an intern at the Harlem Hospital. Your father is so proud of him." She paused, realizing what she'd said.

"No need to worry, Mom. I'm no longer worried about what Dad thinks or does."

"Your brother wants to talk to you. He misses you."

"I miss him, too. I should have kept in contact with him. I was too angry with him when I left."

"I know, I know. I knew you never thought he'd do what his father wanted him to, but he's happy. He loves being a doctor."

"He does? I'm sure it's more about what Dad wants," Tori said.

"Maybe at first. But I promise you, he's doing what he wants to. You should call him."

"Maybe I will."

"I'm sure he'd be happy with that. His birthday is coming up. It may be the perfect time to call him. Go out with him."

"Okay, Mom. I'll think about it. That's all I can promise. I'm sorry, but I have to go."

"Please don't go yet. I have something important to tell you."

"Okay, but you have to hurry. I have a meeting in a few hours. What is it about?" Tori asked.

"I'm thinking about leaving your father."

Tori didn't know what to say, but she knew that

she felt like screaming with joy. She couldn't believe it. She didn't need to say anything. It was best if her mother did the talking.

"I can't stay with him anymore. The women, the drinking, the cruelty. I've done my penance."

Tori tried to respond but she couldn't find the words.

"Don't you have anything to say?" her mother asked.

Tori knew her mother needed strength, needed reassurance. "I'm proud of you, Mom. You sure you're ready for this?"

"To be honest, I'm not sure. But I finally know I want to do it. I've seen both you and Jake make something of your lives. It may be too late to have my dreams, but I want to be my own woman. But I can't do it on my own. I need your support."

"Don't worry about anything, Mom. You let me know what you want and I'll help out."

"I'm coming to New York and staying with Jake. He has his money from his trust fund now, so he's willing to take care of me until I can get a job. I have nothing."

"Mom, you don't worry about anything like that. Do you have a number for Jake? I'll give him a call or go over to where he lives."

They talked for a bit before her mother finally put the phone down. Tori wanted to shout for joy. Her mother sounded different from the woman she'd spoken to just a few months ago. Something had happened to help make that change in her mother.

Tori sat. The stress was too much for her. She headed to the grand piano. She needed to unwind and what better place than where she created the music she loved?

Often at night, when she got home from the nightclub, she'd compose something that she had no control over. At the weirdest time songs would come to her. This was one of those times.

She placed her hands on the keys, feeling the energy that only a composer like herself would understand. The music flowed from within. At times single notes, at times a series of notes. Sometime words came with the music and the restriction of being human forced her to write, then tinker on the piano, then write again until the song became what she wanted it to be.

A new song took shape about a handsome knight in shining armor with a mane of dreadlocks floating around him as he galloped on horseback.

By morning, the song was written.

And for the moment, the overwhelming stress she felt was forgotten.

At six o'clock that morning, Tori closed her eyes, willing herself to sleep, and when she did, the smile on her face remained during her dreams of Barbados and the love she had finally learned to accept.

Her life was going exactly how she'd planned it.

So why wasn't she as happy as she should be?

* * *

Russell returned to New York after spending an additional two weeks in Barbados. The island's lush greenness helped him to start the process of healing. Not that he was tortured or tormented by anything in his life, but it had helped him to reconnect with his family, especially with Shayne.

Each day he'd worked alongside Shayne, learning about running the plantation. He'd finally come to realize how talented his brother was and the magnitude of the work he had to do to keep the plantation successful.

In their time together, they'd grown closer and Russell realized that if he'd seen Shayne not only as a brother, but also as a friend, things might have been different.

One of the things he did learn was that he loved the land and loved his heritage. His pride in his brother jumped threefold and he'd not hesitated to talk to Shayne about his life…and his love.

In his conversation with Shayne, he'd learned so much about himself, because Shayne recognized that, to some extent, they were so alike.

Today, however, Russell made a conscious decision to focus on his work. He and his cameraman would be attending a VIP function to celebrate the restoration of a small but historically significant theater in Harlem.

When he'd been asked to cover the official opening, he'd not been too pleased. On reflection, he realized that working on a feature like this could ease the stench of the other story he was working on.

There was nothing he hated more than wrong-doing, but when the abuse affected the lives of children, his anger boiled.

On the drive to Harlem, Russell turned his thoughts to brighter things. His nephews and nieces came to mind.

Tamara's kids were perfect and he'd spend his last days in Barbados getting to know them. Of course, he'd had to leave time for Darius, who hero-worshipped him, and announced, much to the trepidation of his father, that he planned to put an earring in his left ear for his birthday because he wanted to be just like his uncle. Of course, he brought several of his friends over to see his "cool" uncle who lived far, far away.

Arriving at the theater, Russell immediately saw his cameraman and they proceeded into the building. Leaving Corey to get the shots they'd discussed, he was headed for a seat somewhere in the middle of the auditorium when he felt that someone was watching him.

He scanned the auditorium, only recognizing a few officials from the district, and a few reporters he knew. He nodded but the awareness continued.

And then he glanced up, remembering the boxes, and his heart almost stopped.

Tori sat in one of the boxes, her gaze focused on him.

She smiled, and acknowledged him with a simple wave of her hand.

He nodded, making sure his face was as expressionless as possible. He had no intention of letting her shake the world he was slowly feeling comfortable in again.

He nodded again and then turned his gaze to the entrance, where several familiar prominent black men and women were about to enter.

There was a fanfare of music and then she was forgotten in the flurry of activity when he focused on the task at hand.

During the intermission, he glanced up, but she was not there. He experienced a loss so intense he found himself losing focus. But he soon understood the reason for her disappearance.

When Tori was announced as the next performer, he held his breath.

She came onstage in a dress that flowed around her. She was stunning. The crowd went wild and he found himself standing and clapping with them.

She held the mike and said, "Hi, I'm Tori and tonight I want to do a special song not included on my album. It's a song I wrote for a very special person who's in the audience tonight. The song is called 'A Knight to Remember' and that's K-N-I-G-H-T."

Russell felt as if all eyes were on him, but remembered that no one would know she was talking about him.

Tori walked over to an ivory grand piano and sat gracefully. From the first note, the song captured everyone in the audience and didn't let them go, enchanting them with its sheer beauty.

Russell shifted in his seat, uncomfortable with what was happening. It was not only the words of the song, but the raw emotion in her voice.

He could feel it in every nuance of tone. What bothered him most was that she sang it for him. She'd sung for him before, but now there was something different.

When the song came to an end, she did not move for a few seconds. The applause thundered.

Russell could tell she had not regained complete composure and was close to tears.

When the applause died down, she blew a kiss at the crowd and moved off the stage.

The rest of the celebration continued, but she did not return to her seat.

And then his cell phone vibrated.

He glanced down. A text message.

Please meet me backstage after the concert.
Tori.

Russell knew even before he finished reading the text that he'd go. He couldn't deny that he wanted to see her.

The time moved sluggishly on, and when the emcee thanked everyone, Russell was already walking toward the backstage door. Fortunately, his press pass give him easy access and he was informed that Ms. Matthews had left his name, allowing him admission.

At the dressing room with her name on the door, he knocked, waiting for her to give him entry. When she didn't respond, he pushed the door, entered and closed it behind him.

She sat at the mirror, her back to him, and when their gazes locked in the mirror, she averted her eyes, and continued to clear her face of makeup. "Thanks for coming," she said. "Give me a minute, I'll be done soon."

A few minutes later, she stood, dropping the dress she wore; she wore only a bra and those strips of cloth she called panties. Damn, he missed taking them off her.

He felt his body stir and forced himself to think of other things instead of taking her clothes off.

"I invited you here because I want to talk with you, if it's okay. But I need to take a shower first."

With that she skillfully unhooked her bra and he watched it drop to the floor. Next her panties followed and it took all his willpower not to go to her.

Her little striptease could mean nothing.

She moved toward him without a hint of prudishness.

When she was in front of him, she stood silently. "I'm yours if you want me," she said.

He yearned to strip naked and join her. Instead he pulled her to him and held her tightly, not wanting to let her go.

He knew how much it had taken her to do what she did. Her love for him was evident. With the removing of her clothes she told him she was his.

He felt the sting of tears, but the tears were for her. He'd reduced this woman who loved him so much to this.

"I love you, Tori," he finally said. "I'm sorry. I've been such an idiot. I promise you things will be different from now on."

With that he eased away from her, to see tears pooled in her eyes.

He picked up her clothes and handed them to her. As he watched her get dressed, he was still moved by what had just taken place.

When she finished, he said, "Come with me. Let's spend the night together.

She nodded her agreement and took her hand in his and they walked out together.

Russell groaned.

The dream was an interesting one. His dreams of Tori were all different, but this time he knew a pleasure that curled his toes.

But the dream felt strange and real.

As his eyes opened, he assimilated the fact that Tori was suckling one of his nipples.

What a way to wake up!

They'd not made love when they reached his apartment late that night. They'd left Harlem and had a late dinner at a popular Manhattan restaurant. They'd talked all night and finally fallen asleep in each other's arms.

He raised her head.

"We need to talk," he said.

"I know. So let's talk," she replied as he drew her to him, her head coming to rest on his chest.

"So, what do we do from here? I've learned something tonight. I love you as much as I did a year ago, and I know that whatever we have to do won't be easy, but it doesn't mean it can't be done."

"I love you, too, Russell. You know that. And yes, I want to make this work. It has been good tonight, but relationships aren't just made perfect overnight. We have to work on it."

"Listen, I know how silly I've been. But I want you to put that behind us. Give me a chance to make it right."

"Okay, we'll give it a try, but no more promises. I'm not sure if a relationship right now for me is the best thing, but we'll see how it goes. That's all I can say."

Russell didn't particularly like what she said, but it was all he could ask of her. The rest would have to come. Until then he'd satisfy himself with what he had.

Her love.

With time, commitment would come.

For a moment, they looked at each other; not just looked, but really looked.

He kissed her, gently and tenderly.

Oh, they could make love again soon, but tonight, he just wanted to hold her and let her know how much he loved her.

Russell eventually drifted off to sleep, but Tori couldn't. She felt an excitement and contentment she hadn't felt before. Tonight was a turning point in their relationship and she recognized the subtle change in Russell.

She had taken her clothes off. Yes, she wanted him, but when she'd taken them off in the dressing room, it had definitely not been about sex.

She loved him and she'd wanted him to know at that moment, she was his. She could no longer fight the love she had for him.

When he'd reached for her, not to make love to her, but to hold her, the gesture had moved her to tears.

The Russell she'd seen tonight was the man she loved, the man she wanted to spend the rest of her life with; the man whom she wanted to father her children.

In the time they'd known one another, they'd both changed.

She knew she'd changed. She was stronger, more confident with the woman she was.

Russell turned in his sleep, drawing her closer.

She snuggled up to him.

This was where she belonged.

She sighed, releasing the worries and cares in her life.

In seconds she was fast asleep.

Chapter 14

A few days passed before Russell saw Tori again. Each time he called her, he got the impression that her schedule was packed. And he knew it was. He only had to turn his television on and see her either working the talk-show circuit or in her music video.

Her second single had also made the number one spot on most of the charts across the county and posters of her hung all over the city. Music journalists were claiming her to be a cross between Whitney and Mariah, and he could see why. With Mariah's range and Whitney's soul, the comparison was inevitable. But she handled it with the skill of a professional each time the question was posed to her.

Though her first music video made him proud, a part of it made him realize how lonely he was.

She'd invited him to several functions, but each time he'd had to refuse. His own work was taking up most of his own time, but they chatted often on the telephone. There was a distance and tension between them that made him long for the easy camaraderie they had when they'd first met.

Russell realized something about his life. He didn't have any friends. There were cool guys at the paper, but after work there was rarely any contact with them.

Man, his life was really pathetic.

When he'd first started at the newspaper the guys had invited him out for drinks, but he'd always been too busy studying. Getting his master's had been the most important thing for him.

He strolled into the bedroom. He needed to get some rest. He was sure she would call.

At midnight, he decided to go to bed.

Tamara jumped awake.

Russell.

She needed to talk to him. She glanced over at the clock. Six o'clock. She'd get up and call. In a few hours she'd have to be up anyway. Thursday was a morning she and Kyle went running.

Kyle stirred beside her, coming awake slowly. He reached across for Tamara, but when his hands touched the bed instead of her, he said, "Tamara, what's wrong?"

"I'm not sure," she replied. "You go back to bed. I have to call Russell."

"Okay," he replied, rolling over and going back to sleep.

She didn't need to say any more. Her husband knew about the strange connection she had with her brother.

She rose from where she was sitting, exiting the bedroom. Alex followed her, as expected. He prided himself on being a guard dog as well as Kyle's Seeing Eye dog.

She walked toward the study where Kyle worked, found the phone and dialed her brother's number.

He picked it up on the second ring.

"Tamara, I was thinking about calling you," he said before she could greet him.

"I knew something was wrong."

"I'm okay, just need advice about a few things."

"You mean Tori?"

"Yeah, Tori, but other things, too."

"You want to talk about it?"

"The strangest thing happened to me tonight. I needed someone to talk to and the only two persons I could think about to call were you and Shayne. I realized that I really don't have any friends. I had friends at school, but I've lost touch with them. I remember being at your wedding and sitting with Shayne, Troy, George and Jared and enjoying the bonding. It was the strangest feeling, but I felt like I belonged there."

"I know what you mean. We've spent so much time with our studies, we haven't had time for friends. For me that has changed. Carla and I are the best of friends, and her friend Sandra comes to Barbados so often, the three of us hang out together all the time."

"Sandra. Troy's archenemy?" he asked.

"Oh, yeah, but that's for now. All that bickering and conflict is just a cover for the heat between the two of them."

"Definitely not. They hate each other."

"Haven't you heard? Hate is just the twin brother for love."

Russell laughed. "Well, if what you say is true, I can't wait until the sparks start flying."

"Oh, that will come in time. I want to be sure to be around when the loving starts."

"This love thing is stressful."

"It is but when it's good, it's good. Things between you and Tori will work themselves out."

"I've been seriously thinking about coming back home."

"Finally?"

"Yes, finally, but now my love life is so complicated. I'm not sure I can be there and Tori here."

"Russell, I'm convinced things will work themselves out. You two just need to sit down and talk about the possibilities. Even if you have to live in the U.S., Barbados will still be your home. You'll be able to come home when you want."

"That's true. We'll get some time to talk when the hype for the album cools down a bit. So, how are my nephew and niece doing?"

"They're fine. They're both finally sleeping through the night."

"Good, when are you going back into work?" he asked.

"In a week or two. I've been going in a bit during the week to help with any surgeries, but my assistant is working well on his own."

"That's true. At least you don't have to worry about your practice."

"I don't. I just have to take care of my family. One of these days, you'll have one of your own. With three individuals to take care of plus a husband, my life is complete."

"Three individuals?" he asked.

"Remember, Kyle and I already have an adopted son. He may be just a few years younger than I am, but I'm handling this mothering thing quite well. In fact, Jared is coming to New York for a few weeks this summer. He wants to relax, take in a show or two and do some shopping. It didn't even cross my mind he could stay with you. Legally you're his uncle."

"Lord, I'm beginning to feel like an old man. But no problem, I'll enjoy his company for a few weeks. It's not that anything much is happening in my life. Tori is going on tour in the next few weeks for two months."

"Is that sarcasm I hear in your voice?" she asked.

"Sorry, didn't mean to sound like that. I'm learning to deal with it."

"And here I was thinking that the issues between you two were resolved."

"I'm trying, but it's hard to deal with a woman having something that demands more time than you do."

"You learn to think about the other person first and then about yourself. Love is about selflessness."

"I know all that, but at times, I can't help being jealous, though I'm learning to deal with it."

"Okay, if everything is going fine, I hear my kids crying. I have to go."

"Love you, sis."

"Love you, bro."

It was totally unexpected when Tori finally saw Russell. She was completely bored with what was going on when she looked up and their eyes met from across the room. On reflection, the moment reeked of corniness, but when she saw him, Tori realized something that her heart had tried to bury…she missed this lovely hunk of a man who made life worth everything. In that moment she knew that she wanted the love—unwavering and totally selfless—that he had to offer.

Tori finally realized what her problem was. She'd

been fighting all that Russell had to offer. She didn't even want to deal with commitment and compromise. For too many years she'd fought against all that her parents' marriage had represented.

As Russell walked toward her, she devoured him with her gaze. To her, he looked beautiful. He walked with the slight swagger of hips that always made him look sexy and appealing. His locks were tied back as usual, emphasizing his strong cheekbones and the stubborn tilt of his chin. A gold stud graced one ear.

What she saw in his eyes told her so much. It was one of the things she loved about him. Despite his stubbornness, his eyes made him vulnerable as they revealed his every emotion.

She saw his need and the love that he'd bared his soul to give.

And she'd turned him down to sing.

When he reached her, she did the unexpected. She moved easily into his arms, delighted by the firmness of his body against hers.

A light flashed and she sighed. She'd forgotten the photographers. She could just see the newspapers in the morning.

But she didn't care. She felt at home. Ready to take their relationship to where they both wanted it to be.

"I love you, Russell Knight."

She noticed his hesitation, but it didn't worry

her. She knew him; knew it wasn't easy for him to say how he felt. She had hurt him enough.

When the words did come, there were strangled.

"I love you, too, Tori Matthews. Hopelessly and unwavering. But I think we better go on the dance floor if we don't want to make a spectacle of ourselves. We're famous, you know."

The laughter tickled her ears. At least he still had that quirky sense of humor, another thing she loved about him. She smiled, unable to resist his wit.

"Yes, Russell Knight. Tomorrow morning, our picture will be in every newspaper. Can you handle that?"

He led her to the dance floor, his arms guiding her as he took the lead. "Oh, I can handle anything. I came prepared. If I'm going to be the husband of a celebrity, I'm not only going to have to dress the part, but also be the part, so I made sure I gave them my best side, honey."

His words touched her. Russell, in his own macho way, was telling her that he'd pulled down that great wall that existed between them.

"Something I've learned, Tori, is that any man who puts his pride before his vulnerability doesn't deserve to be loved. I want your love, more than anything I have ever wanted. I've been trying to force our love instead of letting it grow naturally and beautifully."

No wonder he was a writer. His words waxed poetic. She was moved by what he said.

But the chatting came to an end. She gave herself up to the music, resting her head on his chest and feeling the rhythm of the music.

She didn't know what was going on, but there was something profoundly psychological about the moment. So she released all the negativity inside and enjoyed the moment.

In the morning they'd talk, but tonight they would make love and their souls would become one. She knew that tonight the loving would be more than just that.

At the stroke of midnight, Russell sat quietly, his woman's head resting against his chest as she slept.

For the past several hours, they'd sat talking and he felt a calmness of spirit that he'd not felt in years.

Russell closed his eyes and for the first time in years spoke to God. He was blessed and yet he'd not acknowledged his creator for years. He thanked Him for giving him a woman as talented and special as Tori.

Russell knew he'd messed up on more than one occasion, but he realized now that his strength came not because of those alpha qualities he thought made him a man, but because he'd stopped for a moment and recognized his flaws.

Being a man was admitting when you were wrong and doing everything in your power to deal with it.

He'd wanted to love a part of her, and leave

another part behind, but if he wanted to love her, he had to love her completely and unconditionally.

Maybe that's what had been wrong with his life for so long. He'd refused to listen to the music and in the process had ignored the music from deep within him.

Tori stirred, her eyes opened, and then she smiled.

"Russell," she said, raising herself to an upright position. "I need you."

He stopped her, placing a finger against her lips.

He stood, standing before her a man, her man, the man she wanted and the man he wanted to be.

He reached to unbutton his shirt, taking his time, and felt the first spark of excitement as their eyes caressed each other.

He slipped out of his pants next, letting them slide slowly down his hips until they pooled on the floor around his feet.

A white pair of boxers followed and then he stood naked before her; his penis, rock-hard, saluted her.

There was something about the moment. He was proud of his body, but there was something weirdly exciting about standing in front of a woman stark naked with an erect penis.

He felt vulnerable and exposed and as she looked at him with the flame of desire in his eyes, he felt wanted.

Tori reached for him, placing her hands around his buttocks, and pulled him toward her.

She lowered her head, putting her mouth on the firm length of him and startling him with its coolness. She took him completely and caused him to groan with excitement.

Damn, it felt so good.

She worked her tongue until he felt that he was going crazy.

He didn't want this anymore. Release would come too soon, and when he made love to her he wanted it to last.

Russell shifted her, placed her at the edge of the bed, bent his head, and slipped his tongue inside her.

Tori screamed, literally screamed, and he hoped his neighbor hadn't heard.

His tongue worked its magic, bringing her to a frenzy until she give one last groan and her body shuddered with release.

He wasted no time before he knelt and slipped himself inside her. Russell groaned.

She opened her eyes wide, startled by the feel of him.

He took her slowly, working himself in and out of her with a rhythm that he knew would bring her release again.

Russell groaned again, loving the tightness of her vagina around his penis, her muscles contracting and relaxing and giving the ultimate pleasure until it took all his mind control not to reach his orgasm.

When the release did come, it was a wondrous

moment. Holding each other, they welcomed the rush of heat that sent them spiraling into flames of desire.

In that moment they knew they'd taken a step in the right direction. Russell knew that everything was going to be all right.

Russell sat at the breakfast island, watching as Tori scrambled eggs and made grilled hot dogs for them.

He returned his focus to the newspaper. They were right. Two of the papers he'd purchased had an article on the songstress's mystery man.

One actually had a short profile on him and he recognized the name of the reporter. He was going to have to give Steve a call.

But then he realized it didn't make sense. The man was only doing his job, just as he did, and being with Tori made him news.

He laughed.

"What's so funny?" Tori asked.

"I was just thinking about calling a reporter I know who takes photos for a sleaze magazine and realized how silly I was being," he replied. "So, what are your plans for today?" he asked.

"Not sure. Don't want to go to work."

"You want to do something?

"Yes, I want to go see my brother. I know he lives here in New York but I haven't seen him in years."

"You know where he lives?"

"Yes, in Harlem. He's going to med school and lives at an apartment complex near the hospital where he lives. I have his number in my phone."

"Okay, you sure you don't want to call first? Make sure he'll be at home?"

"I prefer to go. I want to surprise him."

"Okay, we'll do that. Today is Sunday, so unless he works Sundays, we should find him home. He'll be happy to see you."

They took their time eating breakfast and then showered and made love with the water cascading around them.

Hours later, as they pulled up in front of a brownstone town house, he reached for Tori's hand. She was cold and he knew she was afraid.

"I'll stay in the car. This is a moment for you and your brother. Come for me when you need me."

"I will."

She exited the car, and walked slowly up to the door of the house.

When she knocked the door opened and her brother stood there, a bit older, but still as handsome as he'd ever been.

The look on his face was almost hilarious, but she couldn't laugh.

"Victoria?"

She didn't have time to reply. Her brother placed his arms around her, and held on to her for dear life.

She felt the wetness and realized that they were both crying.

They separated and they looked at each other.

"So, this is how my sister looks now that she is famous?" he asked.

"No, I'm the same Tori," she said.

"Maybe in some ways, but you're more confident. Stronger. That's what matters. You want to come inside?"

"Yeah, but I have a friend waiting." She pointed in the direction of Russell's car.

"Let him come. We can't leave him out there. We'll talk, really talk another time. What are you doing for lunch tomorrow?"

"Nothing much. We don't start filming my next music video until next month."

"Good, we'll definitely meet tomorrow."

Jake looked toward the car and gestured for Russell to come.

When Russell reached them, Tori introduced them.

Her brother placed his arm in hers and they walked inside.

Russell stood by the window looking out at the city. The lights, on all night, slowly started to flicker off.

Yesterday had been a good day. He and Tori had spent several hours with Jake and he'd listened quietly as they'd made plans to be a part of each other's lives again.

Tori's mother would soon be coming to New

York. She was staying with a friend in Florida for the next few months before she arrived. She'd made the final step and neither Tori nor Jake could contain their delight when they spoke to her on the phone.

Russell smiled. At least they had both dealt with the conflicts in their families and could now focus on each other.

Pulling the box from his pocket, he opened it. A ring twinkled back at him.

He would ask Tori this morning. Strange since people usually did this at night. But to him, mornings were made for romance. The rising sun promised so much with its first rays of sunlight.

Russell heard Tori stir behind him, and for the briefest of moments a wash of apprehension filled him with dread, but he brushed it aside.

He was doing the right thing.

When Tori touched him, he turned to face her.

For a while they looked at each other and then she said, "Russell, I love you."

He smiled, opened his hand and showed her the box he held.

"I love you, Tori Matthews. Will you marry me?" he asked.

Tori didn't hesitate. "Yes, I'll marry you, Russell Knight," she replied.

Russell lowered his head to kiss her.

He was right.

Mornings were the best time for romance.
The best time to start a new chapter in one's life.
He was looking forward to his life with Tori.

Epilogue

Russell Knight and Tori Matthews were married on the island of Barbados, a quiet affair that took place on the grounds of the plantation house. In the background, the soothing rhythms of one of the island's top steel pan orchestras helped to create an atmosphere of romance and love.

Tamara, holding one of her children, watched as her brother and his new wife walked down the pathway, lined with local flowers, dancing in the wind.

Next to her, Kyle sat quietly listening to all that was going on. The memories of her own wedding were vivid in her mind, but today was her brother's day.

Jared, on the other side of Kyle, held the other twin. She glanced at him. She couldn't help but notice how much he'd matured in the two years he'd been away.

The plantation's massive garden, beautifully decorated in tones of pink and white, was the perfect setting for the wedding.

Russell, handsome in a black tuxedo, beamed at the crowd, his stance clearly hinting at the pride he felt. Tamara felt the trickle of tears as the happiness bubbled up inside.

She'd ached for her brother to find someone special. And Tori was definitely that someone. She'd had a good vibe about Tori when she'd visited those months ago, and since her arrival a few weeks ago, she'd grown to love her sister-in-law.

In fact, the whole family loved her. Of course, Tori had been initiated into their circle of friends. They might all live in different places, but the bond between them was already strong.

As Tori and Russell passed, her brother turned in her direction, a broad smile on his face and she knew he would be all right.

The crowd stood, clapping loudly and cheering for the new couple. She turned to her husband and felt an overwhelming desire to touch him, something she did often.

She leaned over and whispered in his ear, "I love you."

Kyle's lips found hers and the gentlest of kisses stirred her.

Even now, the chemistry between them continued to flame and she knew that sometime tonight, they'd have their own romance. She trembled in anticipation.

Glancing across the crowd, she caught a glimpse of George and Troy. She instinctively searched for Sandra. Tamara noticed a strange look on Sandra's face. Following her friend's gaze Tamara realized that Sandra was looking at Troy. And then reality struck. The look on Sandra's face was one of unadulterated lust.

So she was right. There was something there. Tamara smiled. There was another romance in the making. Sandra, her vivacious, brash friend, claimed she hated doctors, but Dr. Troy seemed to have caught her attention.

Tamara had every intention of watching the spark between them fly.

She'd have to chat with Carla. They both loved a good romance and what better romance than a live real one?

Troy and Sandra! She chuckled.

Kyle turned to her. "So, what are you laughing at?"

"Oh, I'll tell you later, but it's definitely most interesting."

That night, in room 224 of the Hilton Hotel, Barbados, Tori Matthews-Knight stood before her husband, naked and flushed with excitement.

Russell watched as she jumped on the bed and straddled him. He'd been ready for this all day and his excitement and anticipation felt as strong as when he'd made love to her for the first time.

He was ready to make love to her, but Tori had something up her sleeve.

In her hand she held a wineglass filled with a gold liquid, which she tilted and poured on his chest.

She put the glass down and proceeded to place her lips on him, raining gentle kisses on his body while licking the wine off him.

When she was done, he reached for her, urging her to lie on her back. When she complied, he took the glass and returned the favor, using his mouth on her until her cries of ecstasy filled the room.

Discarding the glass, he lowered his head to her breasts, immediately recognizing the sweetness of honey. He licked one breast and then the other.

He trailed downward, his mouth teasing her until he reached the core of her womanhood.

His mouth covered the soft mound, and he opened his mouth to give his tongue access to her sweetness.

Tori groaned as he pushed his tongue inside and found the sensitive nub. His tongue flicked it before he suckled on it. Her legs widened, giving him greater access, and he continued to pleasure her.

In the fog and heat of his mind, he heard her voice, "Russell, I need you to make love to me."

He shifted and moved to obey her.

When he entered her, he watched her, loving the look of ecstasy on her face.

Tonight, he would take his time. They had a lifetime before them. Often their lovemaking was fast and wild, but now he wanted to savor it, make it last for as long as possible.

He moved slowly, and the gentle movement of his hips, in and out, in and out, stirred him until he fought to stay in control.

When release finally came, the last thing he thought of before he went over the precipice was that there was no other place he'd want to be.

Tori Matthews-Knight was his life.

His love.

She went looking for treasure…
and rediscovered temptation!

MEET PHOENIX

Book #2 in Romance on the Run

National Bestselling Author

MARCIA KING-GAMBLE

Art expert Phoenix Sutherland vows to remain
professional when her sexy ex-husband joins her
expedition to recover a priceless statue. But it's not
long before the thrill of danger rekindles sparks
of desire neither can resist.

TOP SECRET
ROMANCE ON THE RUN

Available the first week of August wherever books are sold.

KIMANI
ROMANCE

www.kimanipress.com   KPMKG0770808

NATIONAL BESTSELLING AUTHOR

ROCHELLE ALERS

invites you to meet the Whitfields of New York....

Tessa, Faith and Simone Whitfield know all about coordinating
other people's weddings, and not so much about arranging
their own love lives. But in the space of one unforgettable year,
all three will meet intriguing men who just might bring them their
very own happily ever after....

Long Time Coming
June 2008

The Sweetest Temptation
July 2008

Taken by Storm
August 2008

ARABESQUE®

www.kimanipress.com

KPALERSTRIL08